Syama Prasad Mookerjee
His Death in Detention

Syama Prasad Mookerjee
His Death in Detention

A Case for Enquiry

Edited by
Uma Prasad Mookerjee

Introduction
Anirban Ganguly

No part of this publication can be reproduced, stored in a retrieval system or transmitted in any form or by any means, electronic, mechanical, photocopying, recording or otherwise, without the prior permission of the author and the publisher.

Published by
PRABHAT PRAKASHAN PVT. LTD.
4/19 Asaf Ali Road,
New Delhi-110 002 (INDIA)
e-mail: prabhatbooks@gmail.com

ISBN 978-93-90101-96-2
SYAMA PRASAD MOOKERJEE
His Death in Detention
by Shri Uma Prasad Mookerjee

Edition
2025

Price
₹ 400.00 (Rupees Four Hundred only)

© Reserved

Printed at
R-Tech Offset Printers, Delhi

Foreword

For a mother to lose a son and a son so brave and noble—is a tragedy unbearable. But for a mother to write a foreword to a book unfolding the tragic tale of the last days of her beloved son makes the tragedy more poignant. And yet I sit to write and I write with a pen dipped in tears.

I have been overwhelmed by the mass of condolence messages pouring in from far and near. They all ring with sincere sentiments. Innumerable persons, known and unknown, have come to me to console me and by consoling me to console themselves. They all come with a genuine gift of tears and mingle theirs with mine. And as I weep with them, proudly do I feel that the loss of my son is a loss to Mother India.

Death is inevitable. But a death in detention—a detention without trial—is neither normal nor inevitable. Yet, such was the death of my son. Imprisoned by persons whose political activities he had the courage to oppose, surrounded by armed guards till his last moments in the hospital, far away from his near and dear ones, without even one familiar face within his last sight, my gallant son—for whose life many would have offered their own lives—met his tragic end. With what words on his lips, in whose presence, and under whose care and treatment did he depart—even I, his mother, it seems, shall never know. I am filled with horror to think of that last night! They—the official dignitaries—have drawn an iron curtain over the whole mystery. They speak to me of the will of God—and I to hear from their lips the name of God!

But let me not lament here the aching void created in me by the death of my beloved son.

I demanded justice from Shri Jawaharlal Nehru. I asked for an immediate impartial open enquiry into this whole tragic episode, but he has failed and failed miserably. With an air of infallibility, he replied that he could 'only' give his 'clear and honest conclusion' to me. But, unfortunately, the facts so far revealed, and as disclosed in the following pages, unmistakably show that his conclusions have no basis in fact and the official versions bristle with inaccuracies and mis-statements. The Prime Minister of India possibly thinks that truth can be sacrificed at the altar of government policy. But truth, I say, shall prevail.

Out of the facts revealed here arise vital questions of far-reaching effect on the destiny of our motherland.

Had my son, a citizen of India, a member of the house of people, a leader of the Opposition, the fundamental right to enter Kashmir without any obstruction from any quarters?

Was the detention of my son, without any trial, by the Kashmir government lawful and justified?

Are the charges of malafides made by my son himself against the Kashmir government sustainable?

Was the Kashmir government guilty of culpable negligence? Did it do all that should or could have been done by them?

Was there any complicity of the Government of India in this tragic episode?

These are the questions, amongst others, which must be answered and all the facts must be brought to light.

I had long dedicated my son for selfless service to the country, and my son sacrificed his life for the cause of the motherland. He had the courage of conviction to oppose the party in power. Am I to believe that in free India to lead an Opposition is a crime? And yet my son suffered detention till death, as a condemned criminal, with this difference that the criminal gets a trial, but for him there was not even a show of trial. It seems, malice and jealousy of persons in authority, armed by the people with unlimited powers, pursued him persistently, and a huge machine of organised injustice was set against him. But my son's courage proved greater than their malice, stronger than any torment their cruelty could devise. And he shall ever live even in death, for, while thinking of him I cannot but think of those martyrs who had died for the love of God or for a cause—martyrs who had "died on the wheel, in the flames, under the sword, riddled with arrows, torn and devoured by wild beasts."

May the facts so far revealed open the eyes of the doers to their own misdeeds that they may repent, and the people of India judge for themselves and take such action as will, for ever, put an end to this agony of Mother India.

May God be with my country!

77 Asutosh Mookerjee Road
Calcutta
30th July, 1953

JOGMAYA DEBI

Introduction

In the early hours of 23rd June 1953, around 2.30 a.m. Dr. Syama Prasad Mookerjee died in detention at the State Hospital in Srinagar. His illness, suppression of the news of his illness, the delay and lackadaisical attitude towards his treatment displayed by the Sheikh Abdullah government and his lonely death has moved generations to repeatedly ask questions over his sudden and mysterious end. The words of Dr. Mookerjee's grieving mother Jogmaya Devi come to mind. In her foreword to this very book, when it first appeared in July 1953, Jogmaya Devi had written:

> Death is inevitable. But a death in detention—and a detention without trial—is neither normal nor inevitable. Yet, such was the death of my son. Imprisoned by persons whose political activities he had the courage to oppose, surrounded by armed guards till his last moments in hospital, far away from his near and dear ones, without even one familiar face within his last sight, my gallant son, met his tragic end. With what words on his lips, in whose presence, and under whose care and treatment did he depart—even I, his mother, it seems, shall never know.

In her demand for justice from then Prime Minister Jawaharlal Nehru, Dr. Mookerjee's grieving mother had raised a number of questions, which Nehru never bothered to answer. "Am I to believe", wrote Jogmaya Devi in her foreword to this volume, "That in Free India to lead an Opposition is a crime? And yet my son suffered detention till death, as a condemned criminal, with this difference that the criminal gets a trial, but for him there was not even a show of trial." Her lament still rings in one's ears, when one examines the sequence of events that unfolded leading to Dr. Mookerjee's detention and his sudden death. Jogmaya Devi writes, "It seems, malice and jealousy of persons in Authority, armed by the people with unlimited powers, pursued him persistently, and a huge machine of organised injustice was set against him."

Conspiracy it was, and Dr. Mookerjee himself realised it once he was allowed to enter Jammu and Kashmir and then promptly arrested. His entry into the State was, in his own words, 'facilitated' by officials of the Government of India, who must have surely been under political instruction to ensure that Dr. Mookerjee entered the State. In a note found in his brief-case after his death, in which Dr. Mookerjee had jotted down points in 'connection with his application before the Kashmir High Court", he wrote that there was a clear malafide on part of the Sheikh Abdullah government and the Government of India, then headed by Nehru in detaining and imprisoning him in Kashmir. This volume reproduces that disconcerting note in its entirety. Pleading for the Court to intervene since there was a malafide behind the act of arresting him, Dr. Mookerjee wrote:

(2) Conspiracy between the Govt. of India and J&K govt.—the circumstances under which my entry was facilitated by Indian Officials.

One of Dr. Mookerjee's closest political colleagues in the erstwhile Hindu Mahasabha, the one who was instrumental in his meeting Veer Savarkar, barrister Nirmal Chandra (N.C.) Chatterjee (1895-1971), Member of Parliament from Hooghly in West Bengal in the first Lok Sabha, delivered one of the most scathing speeches on 18th September 1953, when the House discussed Dr. Mookerjee's death. On Dr. Mookerjee's written submission that it was a conspiracy between the Government of India, that is the Nehru government and the Government of Kashmir, that is the Sheikh Abdullah government, Chatterjee, arguing that the conspiracy charge was justified told the House, that Dr. Mookerjee, in his last days had not "recorded here something untrue, something fantastic, something unfounded. Not only the government of India did not arrest him for the infringement of the so-called permit system which that government introduced—it did not detain him for the alleged violation of the permit system—but the District Magistrate of Gurdaspur actually escorted Dr. Mookerjee and his party right upto the border, and it seems that he was pushed into the State of Jammu and Kashmir as a result of some understanding or some arrangement between the Government of India and the Government of Jammu and Kashmir State." Neither Nehru, nor his Home Minister K.N. Katju could proffer a satisfactory explanation on why his government acted in this manner. One of Dr. Mookerjee's principal biographers,

Tathagata Roy, for instance, writes in his book 'Life and Times of Dr. Syama Prasad Mookerjee' that the impression that Dr. Mookerjee "was imprisoned for entering Jammu and Kashmir without a permit" is a "canard deliberately spread" by Sheikh Abdullah, "as he had done in a broadcast, for reasons best known to him..."

As one examines details, Dr. Mookerjee's notes and statements by those who were with him, it becomes clear that Nehru had allowed him to be ensnared in Jammu & Kashmir. If the government of India was the permit issuing authority and if Dr. Mookerjee did not have a permit, why was he allowed to enter Jammu in the first place? Jana Sangh leader, Vaidya Guru Dutt who was accompanying Dr. Mookerjee, in his deposition, reproduced in its entirety in this volume, recalls:

> On 11th [May] at Batala [city in Gurdaspur district, Punjab] the local S.D.O. entered our compartment, remained sitting with us and introduced himself to Dr. Mookerjee. But he told him that he had not come to arrest him but simply to escort him through his area. His area was over at Gurdaspur and the S.D.O. of Gurdaspur came and sat by when the first man had left. He went with us up to Pathankot. At Pathankot, the District Magistrate and many other officials were present on the platform but they did not arrest us nor did they speak to us. At about 12 o'clock a message from the District Magistrate, Gurdaspur, come to the place where we have been staying to the effect that he wanted to see Dr. Mookerjee. So he came at about 1 p.m. He informed Dr. Mookerjee that he had received a

message from his Government to allow him and his party to proceed to Jammu, in spite of the fact that Dr. Mookerjee and his party had no permit.

Strangely the District Magistrate of Gurdaspur, "offered help to procure conveyance" for the party and Dr. Mookerjee. One of the subordinate officers, in fact, gave a lift to some of the members of Dr. Mookerjee's party in his own vehicle up to the Madhopur check-post on the border with Jammu. At the Madhopur check-post, the well laid plot further unfolded, with the District Magistrate and his officers being present there and wishing the party a 'good journey'. "The driver of our jeep", recalled Dutt, "had at that time complained that he had no permit to enter Jammu State. We demanded a permit from the District Magistrate. He stated that we should proceed and the permit would follow." So, in good faith Dr. Mookerjee and the party proceeded, only to fall into the trap laid out by Nehru's government on one side and Sheikh Abdullah's on the other. "But when we had traversed half the Ravi Bridge, Jammu Police officers and good many constables were found to be standing there and one Mr. Aziz, Superintendent of Police, Kathua, informed Dr. Mookerjee that he could not proceed further as his government had issued an order prohibiting his entry into Jammu and Kashmir State. A surprised Dr. Mookerjee told him that "he had been allowed by the Indian government to go into the Jammu and Kashmir State and he would proceed to that place..." On this the S.P. Kathua, interestingly was well prepared, he "produced another order from his pocket arresting him."

The conspiracy thus was well planned, Nehru's

government allowed Dr. Mookerjee to travel into Jammu even though he did not have a permit and the Government of India's directive mandated that a permit was required, while the Sheikh Abdullah government arrested him because he had entered the State without a permit, even though, as we shall see, at the time of arresting him, the J&K government did not have the permit rule. Does one need further evidence in support of the contention and belief that Dr. Mookerjee was indeed the victim of a huge and intricately planned conspiracy? To anyone who reads this slender volume edited boldly and with frankness by Dr. Mookerjee's younger brother, Uma Prasad Mookerjee (1902-1997), explorer of the Himalayas, celebrated travelogue writer and well known public intellectual, it will be clear that Dr. Syama Prasad Mookerjee, in his quest for protecting India's unity and freedom became the victim of a deep-rooted and many sided conspiracy, "a huge machine of organised injustice", as his mother put it.

The saga of Dr. Mookerjee's arrest, detention and death thus needs to be recounted, reiterated and kept alive in our national memory, for generations to know, how, he had unflinchingly sacrificed himself so that India could be saved. Uma Prasad's volume gained wide popularity for a while. From papers and letters we see that he had circulated the booklet to eminent personalities across the country, while many others, on hearing of its publication, wrote to him asking for copies. Swami Atmasthananda (1919-2017), the fifteenth President of the Ramakrishna Math and Ramakrishna Mission, who was in-charge of the Ramakrishna Mission Tuberculosis Sanatorium in Ranchi in the 1950s, for instance, in a letter to Uma Prasad wrote that "what has happened [Dr. Mookerjee's death] lies too deep for tears and the loss is irreparable...The cruel hand of Death, should I say, rendered Bengal bereft of a towering personality leaving no compeer, in particular, and India, of a noble patriot, in general..." and asked for copies of the booklet to be sent to the Mission's library and hospital. "We have lost one of our very genuine patrons on whom we depended so much", concluded Swami Atmasthananda, describing the active support and involvement of Dr. Mookerjee with the Ramakrishna's Mission's welfare activities and projects.

The appeal of Dr. Mookerjee's magnetic personality had a national spread. Inventor, entrepreneur and one of the most fascinating technical minds that India has produced, G.D. Naidu (1893-1974) often referred to as the 'Edison of India', in a moving letter from Coimbatore, dated, 6th August, 1953, addressed to Dr. Mookerjee's mother, wrote:

> We read in local Tamil daily about the unfortunate and pathetic demise of Dr. Mukherjee [sic] who was a sun and who came to give light to India. After our country is darkened by his disappearance, I understand that you have given foreword for a pamphlet prepared by his brother Shri Uma Prasad Mukherjee. May I request you to kindly send me a copy of the pamphlet with permission to publish the same in local languages in South India?

Information about this booklet had spread far and wide. The urge to know of how and under what circumstances Dr. Mookerjee had died, the desire to broadcast the truth exercised many leading minds of that era. G.D. Naidu's letter indicates how the entire country was shaken by his sudden death in detention.

The impact of Dr. Mookerjee's death was widely felt; it benumbed ordinary Indians, opinion makers and leaders from across the spectrum. For days and weeks the news of his death, the events leading to his death, the now historic correspondence between his mother and the Prime Minister of India in which she boldly demanded an enquiry, called out Nehru for his callous behaviour and exposed the conspiracy behind Dr. Mookerjee's death was reproduced in a number of magazines and dailies across India.

For instance, S.L. Narayan Bhat, editor of the popular Kannada magazine, *'Rayabhari'*, from Udupi, sent a copy of the magazine to Justice Rama Prasad Mookerjee and in a moving letter to him, wrote that the magazine's issue of 22nd July 1953, had published the letters that were exchanged between Dr. Mookerjee's 'esteemed and revered mother' and the Prime Minister of India. That Dr. Mookerjee was a pan-Indian leader and that the impact of his sudden physical absence was felt, discussed and mourned across the length and breadth of the country is palpable from this letter of the editor of *'Rayabhari'*:

> We in a distant corner of India mourn the sad demise of our national leader Shri Shama Prasad Mukherjee [sic]. The issue referred to above has been widely appreciated by the Kannada reading public as the text of the correspondence has been translated only by *'Rayabhari'*."

That his death had also shocked ordinary Indians and

youth across the country, comes across in a passionate letter by a student, Y.B. Puripallam, from Nellore, dated 10th August 1953, to Jogamaya Devi, addressing her as 'grandmother' and beseeching her to send a photograph of "my uncle (Shyama Babu) which is not available in our province...If you are kind enough to send this with your signature I can everyday pray him for his noble sacrifice and I request him to wish me from 'Veera Swargha' to follow his footsteps...A great loss to you, not only to you but to our country...Really, I wondered perplexed, annoyed and grew angry on this coward meanest step taken by Kashmir government to defeat Syamababu, except death none can have the courage to defeat this Tiger of Bengal..."

That a leader of Dr. Mookerjee's stature, brimming with dynamism, national commitment and the urge to serve India better could meet such a sudden and excruciating end at the age of fifty-two could not be fathomed or explained. His death in detention continues to be one of the darkest episodes in post independent India's history. M.R. Jayakar (1873-1959) eminent educationist, member of the Constituent Assembly and erstwhile Swaraj Party leader spoke for many a nationalist heart when he observed in his tribute to Dr. Mookerjee, "To lie in a prison house locked there by his country's Swadeshi government, by persons with whom he shared power as a colleague, is a fitting termination of a warring life...Let us hope that this incident will make the Government of India realise... the deep enormity of their behaviours, which ignored all the canons of fairness and justice accepted by civilised governments."

Basing his entire attack on facts provided in Uma Prasad's book, N.C. Chatterjee's poignant observation on the manner in which Dr. Mookerjee had died still move those who read it:

> Far far away from his family, far far away from his friends, in the chilling atmosphere of a State hospital at Srinagar died Dr. Syama Prasad Mookerjee. But, he died a hero's death, a true martyr to the cause which he held sacred, the cause of India's unity and integrity which he cherished all his life and for which he sacrificed his life...what adds poignancy to the tragic death is that one of the greatest sons of India was robbed of his freedom, not by a government run by alien usurpers, but by a government which was manned by the children of the soil. The greatest tragedy was that he was kept as a prisoner behind the prison bars, without any trial and he was treated like an ordinary criminal in spite of his serious illness because he loved his motherland deeply and passionately and because he sought in his own way to maintain, the unity of the country, and, if possible, to intensify and strengthen that unity and solidarity.

Contrast this with Sheikh Abdullah's reaction, not only was Abdullah not present at the State Hospital to pay homage to Dr. Mookerjee after his death, he saw to it that the news was clamped down, no journalist was allowed to relay the news before 8.00 a.m. that morning – more than five hours after the death had actually occurred. The AIR (All India Radio) correspondence in Srinagar, for example, had come to know of Dr. Mookerjee's death by 6.00 a.m.

but had to wait till 11.00 a.m. for broadcasting the news. The telephone lines were deliberately disconnected; journalists were told that "all telegraph and telephonic connections between the state and the outside world have been severed." Instructions were also sent to the Indian Telegraph Office in Srinagar "to stop all press telegrams from going. Obviously, the government was interested in suppressing the news for some hours", notes one observer who was present among journalists. The first "press telephonic call was allowed to proceed only at 11.00 a.m."

Some of the hitherto unpublished documents and reports recount how at the Kashmir government's behest, Dr. Mookerjee's body was taken out of the back door of the hospital so that the large crowd which had gathered to have a last glimpse of the body would be deprived of it. Abdullah's animosity was so intense that he let loose National Conference workers to intimidate shopkeepers in Srinagar who had wished to observe a *hartal* by keeping their shops shut in protest at the death of Dr. Mookerjee. A copy of a detailed letter written to the editor of the Hindustan Standard by one S.L. Koul, resident of 4th Bridge, Srinagar besides raising some very pertinent questions, also mentions how "agents of Kashmir government prevented *bazaars* in Srinagar from observing *hartal*." Koul also notes how when asked by a correspondent at the airport, where he had gone to see off Dr. Mookerjee's body, "What are your personal reactions?" Abdullah curtly replied, "I have none."

It has also been recorded by Koul, that a few days after Dr. Mookerjee's death, while addressing a meeting of National Conference workers in Srinagar, Sheikh Abdullah said, "Why make so much fuss about it? It is an ordinary thing. A prisoner has died in jail, what does it matter?" He is reported to have told another meeting, "We did our best to save him and doctors were attending on him day and night. If he is dead what can we do? We are not afraid of any intimidation or threats. We have faced many ordeals and we are not going to be cowed down by anybody or anything." Such was Sheikh Abdullah's obdurate arrogance when speaking or referring to Dr. Mookerjee's death. Addressing a delegation of teachers from Delhi who were on a goodwill mission to the Valley, just three days after Dr. Mookerjee's death, Sheikh Abdullah, said referring to the permit system, that it presented some difficulties, but that "We have to submit to the needs of the national security of India as defence of the country was paramount for every Indian." What was the Sheikh implying? Was he implying that Dr. Syama Prasad Mookerjee was detained because he was a threat to national security? Could there be a more preposterous argument to make against one who had in fact staked his entire political career, his life, for preserving and protecting India's national security and unity?

In fact, as we read in this book, Sheikh Abdullah's government "passed an Ordinance making it an offence for anyone to enter the State without a State permit. But Dr. Mookerjee was not arrested under this Ordinance" since he was arrested on 10th May and the Abdullah government passed the ordinance on 11th May and yet we see Sheikh Abdullah, "in his broadcast talk, after the arrest" declare that "Dr. Mookerjee had been arrested for entering the State without permit." Even after Dr. Mookerjee's death,

Sheikh Abdullah "reiterated the same ground" and said that even though, "the permit system means some difficulty for us, we have to submit to the needs of the national security of India as defence of the country is paramount for every India." Thus, as Uma Prasad Mookerjee contended, "according to the Kashmir Premier, Dr. Mookerjee's arrest was for the 'national security' and 'defence' of India.

A number of reports and witnesses suggest that doctors delayed in treating Dr. Mookerjee. Uma Prasad Mookerjee's volume brings up a number of specific questions on Dr. Mookerjee's death. It clearly delineates a series of events leading to his death, which cannot be explained except by saying that there indeed was a deliberate attempt to entrap and eliminate Dr. Mookerjee.

Curiously enough, during the period when Dr. Mookerjee was incarcerated in Srinagar, especially a few days before and after his death, the city daily saw a number of raucous processions shouting "Pakistani slogans such as—*'Hindusthan Murdabad, Pakistan Zindabad; Foreign Troops quit Kashmir; Sheikh Abdullah Zindabad* etc." This was precisely the mindset and politics that Dr. Mookerjee had set out to confront and decimate. He had foreseen that if left unchecked or unchallenged such a mindset would one day make the region a cockpit for separatism. This struggle against separatism proved to be his last battle.

As seen in Uma Prasad Mookerjee's volume, the dominant Nehruvian establishment made an all-out effort to suppress and then erase, from our collective memory, the reasons that led to Dr. Mookerjee's death and the story of how he was tricked into entering Jammu & Kashmir before being arrested. With his characteristic arrogance,

Nehru refused to heed the pleas of Dr. Mookerjee's mother for an enquiry into the circumstances that led to his death. He also ignored the pleas of leaders cutting across party-lines for instituting an enquiry and stubbornly sought to downplay the death. This volume contains those heart-rending letters that Dr. Mookerjee's aged mother wrote to the Prime Minister of India pleading for an enquiry.

Why did Nehru, the 'epitome' of democratic values and political rectitude disallow an enquiry into such a monumental lapse? Did he have something to hide? Political leaders from across the spectrum were united in their demand for an enquiry into Dr. Mookerjee's death. Former Congress president and stalwart Purushottam Das Tandon (1882-1962), presiding over the Banga Sahitya Sammelan in Prayagraj on 1st July, 1953 "supported the demand for an enquiry into the death" of Dr. Mookerjee, while Jayaprakash Narayan (1902-1979), terming the Kashmir government's behaviour towards Dr. Mookerjee as "criminally negligent" argued that having known the facts from Justice Mookerjee of how Dr. Syama Prasad Mookerjee had died, he had no doubt left in his mind that, "the Kashmir authorities were not only negligent but criminally negligent in looking after Syama Babu's health" and under the circumstances, the least that the "Indian government could do was to institute a proper and impartial enquiry into the whole affair." Jayaprakash Narayan also cautioned Nehru, saying that it did not "seem proper for the Prime Minister to pronounce judgement on such a controversial subject and to attempt to whitewash the guilt of those who seem to deserve severe punishment."

Dr. B.C. Roy (1882-1962), then Chief Minister of West

Bengal, a close friend of Dr. Mookerjee, who had closely collaborated with him during crucial periods of Bengal's history and who had full knowledge and understanding of Dr. Mookerjee's health condition, called for instituting an enquiry "by eminent non-official persons like Dr. M.R. Jayakar or Hriday Nath Kunzru (1887-1978), [widely respected statesman, educationist, parliamentarian, freedom fighter, member of the Constituent Assembly and later Parliament] or a Supreme Court Judge." Such a 'step alone', argued Dr. Roy "could allay mounting public feelings." In his letter to Nehru, Dr. Roy also referred to the public's feeling that the Sheikh Abdullah government was callous towards the medical treatment of Dr. Mookerjee. Pandit Kunzru himself "asked the government of India to officially inquire into the circumstances leading to the death of Dr. Mookerjee in Srinagar." While eminent socialist stalwart, Member of Parliament, H.V. Kamath (1907-1982), called for an enquiry to be conducted "by an all-party committee of Parliament nominated by the Speaker and not weighted by a Congress majority." If Sheikh Abudllah, 'has nothing to hide', said Kamath, "he should welcome the inquiry. If he resists, Parliament should consider the adoption of stern measures against him and his government." Kamath asked Nehru to 'rise above petty personal and party considerations and act quickly' in instituting an enquiry.

Sucheta Kripalani, née Mazumdar, (1908-1974), former Congress leader, freedom fighter and later the first woman Chief Minister of Uttar Pradesh, who was Dr. Mookerjee's close collaborator, especially in the aftermath of partition when he put in great effort in handling the refugee issue also demanded an enquiry. Member of the first Lok Sabha, belonging to the Kisan Mazdoor Praja Party (KMPP), Sucheta Kripalani, in a public meeting in Kolkata on July 23rd, 'demanding an enquiry into the circumstances leading to Dr. Mookerjee's death expressed surprise how a leader like Dr. Mookerjee could die in detention and under such circumstances.' If the government did not institute an enquiry into the matter, Kripalani, argued, people "would believe that there was some mystery in Dr. Mookerjee's death, which the Government of India wanted to hide."

Giving expression to the intense public feeling of that period, N.C. Chatterjee, pointed out how the "demand for an inquiry is not from so-called communalists" but also from eminent persons like Purushottam Das Tandon, Acharya Kripalani, Dr. B.C. Roy and Dr. Jayakar and that "Prime Minister Nehru should realise that there is a deep rooted suspicion in the public mind that his government was as much responsible as the Government of Sheikh Abdullah for Dr. Mookerjee's incarceration in Srinagar." In Parliament, Chatterjee called out both the governments when he said that it was "not merely tragic but it is also mysterious, how the last chapter of Dr. Syama Prasad Mookerjee's life was written in detention in the sub-jail and in the hospital at Kashmir", the public, Chatterjee reminded the House, "feel that both Srinagar and New Delhi had badly bungled the situation." K.R. Malkani, (1921-2003), Jana Sangh and BJP veteran, one of the leading public intellectuals of his era, then editor of the Organiser, writes, that Dr. Ambedkar had remarked on Dr. Mookerjee's death in detention that "even vagrants were sent back to their respective states and not kept in jail" and "demand to know why Sheikh

Abdullah had kept him in jail and not sent him back to Delhi or Calcutta."

Yet Nehru stuck to his refusal to order an enquiry. The entreaties of an entire nation could not move him from his petulant dismissal of the fact that there was foul play, that Dr. Mookerjee was deliberately misled, tricked, ill-treated and finally consigned to the jaws of death. Nehru refused to accept the stark reality that, by allowing Dr. Syama Prasad Mookerjee to die, he had presided over the most monstrous undemocratic act since independence. He certainly had something to hide, some truth to suppress, some fact to dilute and erase.

A number of points and issues pertaining to Dr. Mookerjee's death continue to raise questions over the circumstances that led to it. These are issues that give credence to our stand that his death was unnatural and that there was a deep layered conspiracy behind it. It suited certain elements, especially those who wished Kashmir to be separated from India, to see Dr. Mookerjee eliminated, at least this is what one is led to infer when reading or reflecting on his death.

Why was it that when Dr. Mookerjee's personal belongings were returned by the Kashmir government, his personal diaries were missing. Dr. Mookerjee's elder brother, Justice Rama Prasad Mookerjee sent an urgent telegram on 28th June 1953, that is about a week after Dr. Mookerjee's death, to Bakshi Gulam Mohammed (1907-1972) then deputy premier and home minister of the state asking him to "please send immediately Syama Prasad Mookerjee's personal diary and manuscript writings not sent with the body and any other personal belongings that are still there." In a follow up letter to Gulam Mohammed, Rama Prasad provided the specification of Dr. Mookerjee's diary, it was a diary he had been regularly keeping and which was with him in detention in Srinagar, "It is a black bound book." Rama Prasad also specified the other objects that Syama Prasad possessed and which ought to have been returned with the body, "he had also been writing some literary work there. The diary and the manuscript writings have not been sent with his other belongings that came with the body..." Earnestly requesting Bakshi Gulam Mohammed to give his 'personal attention' to the matter, Rama Prasad observed that 'particularly the diary and the manuscript' must be sent 'without fail'. Bakshi Gulam Mohammed's curt reply to Justice Mookerjee's earnest reply was that "all personal belongings of Syama Prasad Mookerjee [was] carried by Tek Chand, his personal secretary and Mr. Trivedi, his Counsel; please contact them..."

On 3rd July 1953, Justice Mookerjee once again wrote to Bakshi Gulam Mohammed, that he was 'greatly surprised' at his reply. "As I said before, the personal belongings that were sent by you with Syama Prasad's body," he wrote, "did not include his diary and mss Writings [manuscripts]. Syama Prasad, we know, had been regularly keeping his diary while in detention at Srinagar. It must have been with him at the Hospital. It is most surprising and regrettable that it was not sent along with his other belongings." Rama Prasad informed Bakshi Gulam Mohammed that "Messrs. Tek Chand and Trivedi informed us that they had brought only those articles that had been made over to them by the Kashmir authorities" and that "some articles had been handed over to Mr. Trivedi at the Hospital but they did not contain the diary." Rama Prasad reiterated his point that Dr. Mookerjee had been writing 'a good deal in detention' and it was curious therefore that the articles sent by Bakshi Gulam Mohammed did not include any of his manuscripts. Needless to say, the 'black bound book' was never found, nor were Dr. Mookerjee's manuscripts traced. The Sheikh Abdullah government tried to apportion the blame of their disappearance on two of Dr. Mookerjee's most trusted lieutenants.

As per witnesses, there was a fountain pen and a half drafted letter in Bengali on the table beside Dr. Mookerjee's hospital bed when he died. That letter too disappeared without trace. That Dr. Mookerjee was in the habit of maintaining a personal diary has been corroborated by Justice Rama Prasad Mookerjee. His diaries written during the 1940s were later published in 2001 and the originals are still preserved. How did the diaries that he maintained during his detention vanish without a trace, why did the Kashmir government refuse to acknowledge that these diaries existed among Dr. Mookerjee's personal belongings, what did they contain? Dr. Mookerjee must have recorded the details of his agonising last days, of the state of his health, his thoughts both political and spiritual—as he was inclined to do, did he also record the humiliation and discrimination that he must have faced? Did it contain information that would have exposed the Nehru-Abdullah nexus, the conspiracy behind his detention?

Of the diaries and missing manuscripts Uma Prasad says that "more light would certainly be thrown on the tragedy if Dr. Mookerjee's diary and other writings were available for scrutiny." These had certainly existed, since, as Uma Prasad also writes, "Dr. Mookerjee in his letters had repeatedly mentioned that he had been spending his time in detention in reading and writing. He used to also write his diary regularly and his fellow detenus testify that he kept the habit in the sub-jail." When he was removed to the hospital, observed Uma Prasad, "Dr. Mookerjee must have taken his diary, if not his other writings, with him" and yet these were not sent "back by the Kashmir government to his family with his other belongings." "There is naturally a strong suspicion," he concludes, "that these writings, and particularly the diary, have been deliberately withheld..."

A look at the various documents in the book makes us realise the shocking callousness displayed towards treating Dr. Mookerjee in his last days. It certainly gives rise to suspicion that the neglect was deliberate and pre-meditated. Umashankar Muljibhai (U.M.) Trivedi (1904-1984), Jana Sangh Member of Parliament from Chittor in the first general elections of 1951-52, close associate of Dr. Mookerjee who had studied law at Lincoln's Inn 'at about the same time as' Dr. Mookerjee, and was his Counsel for appealing to the Kashmir High Court for his release, in a statement on the last days of Dr. Mookerjee, the delay in treating him, his death, the rude manner in which the Kashmir government conveyed it to Dr Mookerjee's family, the manner in which the body was not allowed to be brought to Delhi, not allowed to land in Jullunder and then via Adampur and Kanpur, after repeated delays, was finally directed to Calcutta, gives a detailed insight into those last agonising days in Kashmir. Trivedi who was in Kashmir at that time, and had meetings with Dr. Mookerjee, under restrictions, over a few days, in order to discuss the case and the plea, has, through his account, left for posterity a detailed narration of the events leading to Dr. Mookerjee's death and thereafter. Uma Prasad's book carries it fully. So casual were the doctors treating Dr. Mookerjee in Srinagar, that they failed to even send a death certificate with the body. Justice Rama Prasad Mookerjee's undertaking and the support of the Calcutta Municipal Corporation sorted out the last minute hitch before the cremation.

The main pointers on the situation surrounding Dr. Mookerjee's death that emerge from Trivedi's statement and from that made by one of Dr. Mookerjee's co-detenues Vaidya Guru Dutt, clearly indicate that there was a deliberate attempt to weaken him. For instance, Dr. Mookerjee suffered a heart attack in the early morning of 22nd June and yet he was not removed to the hospital immediately. Instead he was shifted to the hospital a good seven hours after the attack. Even when he was taken to the hospital, he was made to walk, there was no ambulance and he was 'carried in a small taxi and in an uncomfortable position'. The hospital was 'about 10 miles away from the Sub-Jail' and it was astounding that a 'patient suffering from coronary troubles was taken in such a car under such conditions for such long distance'. Even after he was admitted to the hospital, immediate medical relief was not administered to Dr. Mookerjee, and most surprisingly he was not admitted in any ward of the hospital—or to the Nursing Home Ward as claimed, he was kept in a small, unkempt and stuffy room in the Gynaecological Ward of the State Hospital!

Even in the hospital Dr Mookerjee continued to be guarded by a posse of policemen. Vaidya Guru Dutt, in his statement tells us how 'two days previous to the last illness, Dr. Mookerjee had lost appetite and was taking very little food.' On two days prior to his belated removal to the hospital he just took 'two cups of vegetable soup and one or two cups of tea and a cup of coffee in a day' and yet no serious attempt was made to diagnose his illness, or his progressive weakening and loss of appetite. Everyone who saw him during that period was struck by his weak and tired demeanour. Pandit Prem Nath Dogra, who was allowed to travel from Jammu to Srinagar on 19 June 'to meet him, was also struck by his poor state of health and low appetite', recounts Tathagata Roy. Roy further observes that when Prem Nath Dogra asked Dr. Mookerjee the reason for his weakened state of health he was 'informed that it might be due to lack of exercise'.

From records and description of the cottage in which Dr. Mookerjee was detained, Uma Prasad points out that the "size of the bungalow with its compound was very small. There was not even accommodation for a fourth man, and when Pandit Prem Nath Dogra arrived on 19th June, one of the detenues, in order to accommodate Pandit Dogra, had to shift to a tent, specially pitched outside the building." There was inadequate space for walking within the compound, which was overgrown with weeds. Walking was Dr. Mookerjee's principal exercise and the lack of it was making him lose his appetite. "His request for permission to have a stroll for an hour outside the compound was refused." Ten to twelve armed guards were on watch over him every day. "There are armed guards watching day and night. I am completely cut off from the world outside," he wrote in a letter, on 21st May. Lack of exercise, loss of appetite, weakness and an increasing 'pain in the right leg' kept him increasingly confined to the bed and yet no remedial measure were taken to lighten the burden of confinement.

The Organiser, in an article in July 1953, which Uma Prasad has appended in this volume, describes the derelict cottage in which Dr. Mookerjee was detained, "It is neither fine, nor a bungalow. It is a ramshackle cottage. It is not a government building. It is a private house. But it is so desolate and derelict that no tourist has ever cared to hire it. It is unfit for human habitation." Contrary to what the Sheikh Abdullah government put out, the cottage was not situated on the banks of the Dal Lake, "It is not even on the main road. The surroundings are as wild as they are weird... The house itself is full of owls and snakes. Abdullah put a few rickety cots into this reeking house", for Dr. Mookerjee and his companions to stay. This is how a former union minister and a sitting Member of Parliament was treated!

The spot where the cottage once stood in Nishat Bagh area of Srinagar is still fairly isolated. The forbidding mountains rising behind it, continue to give the place a cold and desolate look. The house, the Organiser article, tells us, was 'exposed to gusts of snowy winds from the surrounding the mountains', though the cottage has long since been demolished, the snowy winds still blow from the mountains, giving the place lonely look. Dr. Mookerjee did not have blankets, after complaining of the cold for quite a while, an overcoat and few blankets were sent for the detenues. "The cold and desolation of the place soon affected his health. He complained of pain and sickness to the jail authorities. But the only medical attention he got was from a sub-assistant surgeon in-charge of the sub-jails of Srinagar. So that in the beginning he was treated no better than hundreds of other prisoners."

To add to his woes, each of his letters home, were censored, some of them were withheld and were later sent back with his body. Dr. Mookerjee was being clearly treated as a dangerous criminal and not as one of the tallest nationalist leaders of his era. Sheikh Abdullah's allergy and pettiness towards him and Nehru's disdain for his stature indeed found dangerous expressions.

"There was only one lavatory—accessible through the room used by Dr. Mookerjee and this was used by the other two detenues also, Dr. Mookerjee's room had to be used as a passage." There was no means of communication for those in the dilapidated cottage, "the nearest telephone was in the Water Works Office Building—some distance away from the sub-jail, and being outside the compound was not accessible to nor meant for the detenues..." We are also told that "none of his fellow detenues were permitted to be by his bedside when he was removed to the hospital" and "even after Dr. Mookerjee expressed the desire that his fellow prisoners should be brought to the hospital, no information was sent to them till he passed away."

Dutt notes, that "In spite of Dr. Mookerjee's protest based on competent medical advice during his previous illness at Calcutta, streptomycin was administered to him without a previous pathological examination or without consulting his Calcutta doctors who were available on the phone." An elementary sense of medical diligence for a stalwart like him would have demanded that he be released immediately, or if he was not in a position to travel one would have expected the Kashmir government to inform the Government of India, the Prime Minister, leading to the formation of a medical board and the immediate enlisting of the support of Dr. Mookerjee's doctors in Kolkata. But nothing of the sort was done. His illness, treatment and death was as though hurried through, it was as if, each event was so arranged or planned that it led to the ultimate unravelling.

From Trivedi's statements we realise that 1) despite having had a heart attack on the 22nd June morning, Dr. Mookerjee was not advised to take rest, 2) "he was not immediately removed to the hospital while seven valuable hours were lost", we read in Uma Prasad's summary of the events and situation graph of Dr. Mookerjee's illness that even after this "no laboratory tests or pathological examinations were made as long as Dr. Mookerjee was in the sub-jail" i.e. the decrepit cottage, and even when he was taken to the hospital no X-ray or tests were done on him. Despite diagnosing that he had suffered a heart attack of the 'coronary type, his family was not informed'. Strange behaviour! Isn't it? Did this not display that both Sheikh Abdullah and Nehru had thrown to the winds the basic canons of humanity and justice? Sheikh Abdullah knew, as admitted by him later, that Dr. Mookerjee had a weak state of health throughout the detention, do we then have to believe that the Prime Minister of India did not know of this? Could the state of health of a former Union Minister, a former Member of the Constituent Assembly, a sitting Member of Parliament and the unofficial leader of the

Opposition, not become a source of concern for leaders of India's then ruling party? 3) "immediate medical relief was not made available even after [Dr. Mookerjee's] entry into the hospital, 4) "the gravity of the illness was not noticed," 5) The Superintendent of the Jail deliberately wasted time in removing Dr. Mookerjee to the hospital.

One of the leading doctors of the era, Dr. Naliniranjan Sengupta, who was well acquainted with Dr. Mookerjee's health conditions, having analysed the medical reports through the Kashmir government's communiqué, observed that "to keep a man so obviously ill with such a fatal illness [coronary thrombosis, as he had diagnosed it] in charge of people who cannot even diagnose such severe attacks and if diagnosed, handle him so roughly like a quack, is a blunder which definitely cost the patient's life and cannot be condoned or pardoned." But Nehru was beyond reproach; he never held himself accountable, on Dr. Mookerjee's death he turned a deaf year to all pleas, analysis and conclusion except his own.

The authorities and doctors who were handling Dr. Mookerjee's treatment could have requisitioned the expertise of the doctors who were stationed at the Army Hospital in Srinagar. But this was delayed and by the time a group of senior army doctors led by one Colonel Moitra, Major Mehta and Dr. Chopra arrived, Dr. Mookerjee had already passed away. There is another curious and crucial point in this entire episode, the timing of Dr. Mookerjee's death—even here we see a stark discrepancy. The official communiqué by the Kashmir government stated that he had passed away at 3.40 a.m. on the morning of June

23rd, whereas Vaidya Guru Dutt says, that when they were coming out of the room after having a look at Dr. Mookerjee's body, one of Dr. Mookerjee's co-detenues and attendant in the sub-Jail, Tekchand Sharma, asked a "nurse who had followed us into the room, "at what time Dr. Mookerjee expired". The nurse replied at 2.30 a.m. She also added that Dr. Mookerjee, at about 1 p.m. expressed his wish to have his companions with him."

Who were beside Dr. Mookerjee's bedside at the time of his passing? Was he all alone when he passed away? When did he actually pass away? Why was there a discrepancy in the time given out? How could even this be treated so casually, or was it because there was something to hide and a credible story had to be scripted? Why were not Dr. Mookerjee's colleagues and companions informed when he wanted to see them? Why was every request that he made denied? Why were high doses of streptomycin injected into him despite his protests? Why did the doctor treating him—if at all treatment it could be called—Dr. Ali Mohammed not pay heed to Dr. Mookerjee's point that he had been told 'not to take streptomycin because it does not suit his system' and injected large doses of it a number of times into Dr. Mookerjee? What was the 'white powder' he was being given? No document or record remains for us to make an assessment and whatever can be surmised is from eye-witness accounts that have been recorded. Why did the Jail Superintendent refuse permission for at least one of Dr. Mookerjee's colleagues to stay with him in the hospital? Vaidya Guru Dutt, recalled, "I asked the Superintendent of the Jail to allow us to stay with Dr. Mookerjee in the hospital. At least one of us should be allowed to remain with Dr. Mookerjee in the hospital. He said that it was not possible."

In his dying moments no doctor was on attendance on Dr. Mookerjee. Dr. Ali Mohammed did not live in the hospital premises and one junior Dr. Zutshi, who was filling in for Dr. Mohammed, was in his quarters. There were no specialists who were on attendance that night, and when the doctors came it was too late. The nurse who was attending on Dr. Mookerjee, Rajdulari Tiku, recalled how the dying leader "cried in agony for a doctor but none was at hand..."

Tathagata Roy, makes one, crucial point, it was one last and most decisive episode of the entire sordid saga, that indicates that Dr. Mookerjee's death was unnatural and that there was a pre-planned plot to effectuate it. Roy, who had met Dr. Mookerjee's elder daughter Sabita Banerjee in 2010, recounts how sometime after Dr. Mookerjee's death, Sabita and her husband Nisith and their children managed to visit Kashmir. The Kashmir government, for years had resolutely prevented anyone associated or linked to Dr. Mookerjee from visiting the state. An earlier attempt by Dr. Mookerjee's son, Anutosh had failed. Sabita had succeeded because she had to mention her husband's name instead of her father's in the application form that had to be filled up by those who intended to visit Kashmir.

Sabita succeeded in tracking the whereabouts of the nurse, most probably Rajdulari Tiku, who was on duty the day Dr. Mookerjee died. On the last day, as the doctor, Ali Mohammed, we presume, was about to leave he instructed the nurse, that "whenever Dr. Mookerjee woke up he was to be administered an injection, for which he left an ampoule with the nurse." After sometime Dr. Mookerjee woke up, he was distressed and weak, and the nurse, following Dr. Ali Mohammed's instruction, pushed the injection into Dr. Mookerjee. "As soon as she did it, Dr. Mookerjee started tossing about, shouting at the top of his voice, *"Jal jata hai, humko jal raha hai"* (I'm burning, I'm burning)." The nurse rushed to the telephone, "to tell the doctor and ask for instructions." The reply she got was, *"theek hai, sab theek ho jaiga"* (It is all alright, he will be alright). Meanwhile, Dr. Mookerjee had collapsed 'into a stupor' and that was the end of him." A painful and agonising end it was. Dr. Zutshi, the resident doctor came in followed by Dr. Ali Mohammed, but by then the curtains had fallen on a momentous life. After this meeting, when she returned the next day to carry on the conversation with the nurse, Sabita could find no trace of her. When Roy met Sabita Banerjee in 2010, she was already in her mid-eighties, it was her last interview of sorts, and she passed away soon after.

What did the ampoule contain? Why did Dr. Mookerjee's life end with such an excruciating feeling of being burnt? Was there a prescription? Why was the Kashmir government communiqué silent on it? Since 22nd June was a crucial night with Dr. Mookerjee's condition being delicate, why had the doctors left? Why were the nurse's frantic calls being responded to in such a casual manner?

Dr. Mookerjee's close political associate and Jana Sangh stalwart Balraj Madhok (1920-2016), who was also his first biographer, in a letter dated 24th August 1953, gave another version of Dr. Mookerjee's last hours. Arguing that his version is based on 'true facts about his

[Dr. Mookerjee's] death' which he was able to 'gather from authentic and original sources', Madhok writes that "at 1 a.m. Dr. Ali Mohammed came to him [Dr. Mookerjee] and wanted to give him an injection. Dr. Sahib [Dr. Mookerjee] told him that he was feeling much better and that he did not feel like taking any injection at that time. But the doctor insisted on giving him the injection as a 'precautionary measure'. According to Madhok, the "Doctor left immediately after giving the injection and soon after Dr. Mookerji [sic] began to perspire heavily and his heart began to sink." The nurse on duty, "repeatedly telephoned to the doctor and told him that Dr. Mookerji's condition has become serious. But the doctor Ali Mohammed did not pay any heed to her and he did not turn up till after Dr. Mookerji's death which took place at 2.35 a.m. and not at 3.40 a.m. as given out by the Kashmir govt..." Madhok also mentions the 'precautionary measure' part in his widely read biography of Dr. Mookerjee, "Portrait of a Martyr", that had first appeared in 1969 with a foreword by Vaidya Guru Dutt.

What had been injected into Dr. Mookerjee as a 'precautionary measure' we will perhaps never come to know, but that Dr. Mookerjee was deliberately done away with, and that there was wilful negligence in treating him becomes evident when one goes through Uma Prasad's book, its documents, analysis and the various other papers and letters which have not been hitherto published.

It is difficult to believe that the Prime Minister of India, Jawaharlal Nehru, did not know of Dr. Mookerjee's health condition and even then, did nothing to intervene to get him released. On 24th May 1953, both Nehru and his Home Minister K.N. Katju visited Srinagar for 'rest' and yet, as Madhok records, "They had not the courtesy and decency to visit their august prisoner and see how he was treated there." While Nehru "rested" in style in Srinagar, as a guest of Sheikh Abdullah, Dr. Mookerjee remained in detention, in a derelict cottage, cramped, cold, weakening and abandoned. Is it to be therefore believed that the Prime Minister of India, Jawaharlal Nehru, had no inkling of what Dr. Mookerjee was going through? Nehru himself was often devoid of courtesy or grace, especially when it came to dealing with his political opponents and it was visible in the manner in which he behaved vis-à-vis Dr. Mookerjee's detention, while in Srinagar.

Among some of the papers connected to Dr. Mookerjee's death, we come across a handwritten letter, by one R.R. Sharma, who identifies himself as the 'second steno of Sheikh Abdullah', addressed to Justice Mookerjee, and dated 19th July 1953. Sharma's letter makes for interesting reading:

> You would be surprised to see this letter from an unknown person, but circumstances have compelled me to send you this letter in a very dramatic manner. I have come down from Srinagar to drop this letter to you from Indian soil that is to say from Pathankot that also from Railway Mail Service in train going towards North. This is only to ensure that firstly it reaches you safe, secondly to avoid detection of Police in Jammu and Kashmir. (2) I have very secretly managed and have stolen the entire correspondence relating to Dr. Shama

Pd's [sic] Death between Shri Nehru and Sheikh Abdullah, this is of great importance. File does not only contain the letters, but entire medical original history sheet and treatment and mixtures given to late Doctor Sahib at different stages. Medical officer who has written the prescription in his own handwriting will surely convince you about the negligence and improper treatment. There are so many documents which will lead you to great astonishment... (3) The only difficulty for me is as to how, should I reach at yours in this connection...?

We have no further information of what transpired? Did Sharma, who wanted Justice Mookerjee to arrange for him to come to Calcutta to handover the file and return the same day, since he was already being suspected, eventually manage to deliver the file? Was Sharma's claim true? Did he actually manage to access the file? Was he a genuine person? Sharma ends his letter with, "rest in my next..." and the address given is "C/o Station Master, Panthankot." Did Justice Mookerjee get in touch with him? Did he reply? Was there a second letter?—are all questions we will never come to know. There is no trace of the second letter and there is no one alive today who can throw light on that file of correspondence between Nehru and Abdullah or on Sheikh Abdullah's second steno "R.R. Sharma."

The laments of Dr. Mookerjee's mother, were the most heart-rending. Her letters to Nehru will go down in history as evidence of how intolerant and coldly autocratic the Nehruvian establishment was. In her reply to Nehru who had sent in his condolences, Jogmaya Devi, wrote, "I am not writing to you to seek consolation. But what I demand of you is Justice...His death is shrouded in mystery. Is it not most astounding and shocking that ever since his detention there, the first information that I, his mother, received from the Government of Kashmir was that my son was no more, and that also at least two hours after the end?"

To her appeal for an enquiry, Nehru's imperious response was, "I have since enquired further into it from a number of persons who had occasion to know some facts. I can only say to you that I have arrived at the clear and honest conclusion that there is no mystery in this and that Dr. Mookerjee was given every consideration..." Nehru also did not fail to remind Jogmaya Devi rather brazenly, that he too had spent time in prisons all over India, and therefore knew "something about how a prisoner feels and what the conditions of his imprisonment usually are." In effect, it meant that Nehru had satisfied himself that it was a satisfactory situation and that therefore everyone else, the entire country, Dr. Mookerjee's grieving mother, had to satisfy themselves by subsuming themselves in that supreme Nehruvian satisfaction!

Jogmaya Devi's final response to an unmoving Jawaharlal Nehru was poignant, full of pathos and tragic:

> I had clearly told you that I had positive evidence to prove certain very relevant and important facts. You do not care to know or look into them. You say that you had enquired "from a number of persons who had occasion to know some facts." It is strange that even we—the members of

his family—are not regarded as persons who can throw at least some light on the matter! And yet you call your conclusion to be 'honest'...Your experience in jails is known to us. It was at one time a matter of great national pride with us. But, you had suffered imprisonment under an alien rule and my son has met his death in detention without trial under a national government..."

N.C. Chatterjee echoed the voice of the majority, when he cautioned a stunned and silent House, that "the greatest menace to democracy is the feeling that a political opponent of the government can be liquidated in prison when he is held in detention without trial. That suspicion should be removed. That can be removed only by an honest inquiry..." But Nehru, had dug in his heels, his vain sense of self-righteousness blinded him to the enormity of the crime committed under his watch.

For the first time in 67 years after his death, Dr. Mookerjee's death anniversary this year (23rd June, 2020) and birth anniversary (6th July 2020) will be observed and celebrated in an India freed of the vexatious and divisive Article 370, in Jammu and Kashmir in which only one flag flutters—the Indian Tricolour, reminding us of Dr. Mookerjee's words uttered decades ago in the midst of the struggle for the integration of Kashmir, "It is the question of one flag for the whole of India, India that includes Kashmir."

Prime Minister Narendra Modi's firm determination, the long years of struggle undertaken by legions of workers and leaders of the Jana Sangh, Rashtriya Swayamsevak

Sangh and the Bharatiya Janata party, Union Home Minister Amit Shah's firm administrative sense and Parliamentary strategy and the support demonstrated by the people of India for a united country from Kashmir to Kanyakumari, has seen the fulfilment of Dr. Mookerjee's dream. It has finally sounded the bugle of victory over his final battle. Prime Minister Modi's vision of a new Jammu and Kashmir and Ladakh, is a tribute to Dr. Mookerjee's vision of a united India, and a great India, an India which he dearly and unconditionally loved and revered and for whose sanctity and integrity he ultimately laid down his life.

The story of Dr. Syama Prasad Mookerjee's life and contribution must be narrated to every generation of Indians, but the story of his death in detention must also be told, and passed on from generation to generation, so that it instils determination in very Indian and inspires each one of us to strive to protect, preserve and uphold India's unity and sovereignty. The saga of his death must be recounted so that it reminds us of the extreme political perfidy and pettiness resorted to by a certain self-arrogating group of leaders for whom democracy, liberalism and India's unity and freedom were a convenient façade to camouflage an intolerant and divisive political mind-set and agenda. Such leaders had existed in that era, in which Syama Prasad strode like a colossus, they continue to exist even now, when the vision of a New India is at last finding expression under Prime Minister Narendra Modi.

By re-issuing Uma Prasad Mookerjee's volume, which had long been out of print, Prabhat Prakashan has paid one of the finest tributes to Dr. Syama Prasad Mookerjee.

I hope that this book is widely disseminated and read, that it generates debates and keeps alive in our minds the saga of Dr. Mookerjee's sacrifice. This second edition must not be allowed to sink away or recede. Our efforts to ensure that it reaches every corner of the country will be our most poignant tribute and salute to Dr. Syama Prasad Mookerjee's great life and to his selfless sacrifice.

—Dr. Anirban Ganguly

15th June, 2020
New Delhi

Select References

- Uma Prasad Mookerjee, edited, *Syama Prasad Mookerjee: His Death in Detention – A Case for Enquiry*, Kolkata: A Mukherjee & Company Ltd, 1953.
- Balraj Madhok, *Portrait of a Martyr: Biography of Dr. Syama Prasad Mookerjee*, Bombay: Jaico, 1969, (reissued 2001, New Delhi: Rupa & Co).
- Craig Baxter, *The Jana Sangh: a biography of Indian Political Party*, Pennsylvania: University of Pennsylvania Press, 1969.
- Tathagata Roy, *The Life and Times of Dr. Syama Prasad Mookerjee*, New Delhi: Prabhat Prakashan. 2012.
- *Dr. Syama Prasad Mookerjee*, New Delhi: Lok Sabha Secretariat, 1990.
- *Demand for Enquiry into The Detention and Death of Dr. Syama Prasad Mookerjee: Speech by Shri N.C. Chatterjee*, M.P. in the House of the People, on Friday,

18th September, 1953, [publisher not mentioned]

- *Syama Prasad Mookerjee, Leaves from a Diary*, New Delhi: Oxford University Press, 1993.
- Prashanto Kumar Chatterji, *Syama Prasad Mookerjee and Indian Politics*, New Delhi: Foundation Books, 2010.
- Syama Prasad Mookerjee Papers, Nehru Memorial Museum & Library, New Delhi.

Contents

His Last Days

Review of facts so far revealed

Dr. Syama Prasad Mookerjee died at Srinagar in the early hours of 23rd June, 1953, while in detention without trial under the Jammu & Kashmir government. The news of his death stunned the country—it was so shocking and so sudden! What were the circumstances that led to the loss of so precious a life, everybody asked. But there was none to answer. No official bulletin about his illness was published before his death by the government responsible for his detention. An official statement giving the doctors' bulletin was subsequently released by the Kashmir government. A statement made by the Minister of Health and Jails, Kashmir, was published on 2nd July. The facts as disclosed in these two only official versions seemed to be incomplete, inconsistent and inaccurate. Stray statements of Sheikh Abdullah and a belated statement of Mr. Nehru were of no help to form a complete and correct picture. They merely stated their own conclusions based only on the official version. Mr. Nehru's reference to enquiries "from a number of persons who had occasion to know some facts" does not disclose either the 'facts' or the 'persons'. The result has been that far from throwing any light on the mystery that hangs over the whole affair, these official bulletins and statements have intensified public misgivings. There has been a widespread and persistent demand for an immediate impartial enquiry into the matter. But nothing has yet been done to meet this demand. The purpose of this review is to present before the public a dispassionate review of some of the facts as revealed in Dr. Mookerjee's letters to the members of his family and other documentary evidence that has come into their hands.

They throw much light on the events leading to his arrest, detention and on his treatment in jail, his state of health and illness in detention. These facts, all supported by documentary evidence, throw a challenge to the official statements issued by the Kashmir government and claim to demolish the very basis of the opinion held by Mr. Nehru. The public can judge for themselves how the tragic end came and what importance should be attached to the propaganda carried on by the governments of India and of Kashmir with a view to shirking an independent, impartial enquiry.

Some of the relevant documents that could not be incorporated in the review itself have been given in the Appendix for ready reference. Passages quoted from letters written in Bengali are literal translations from the original.

I

CIRCUMSTANCES LEADING TO THE ARREST

His arrest, the grounds of his detention and the conduct of the Government of India

There is a general impression that Dr. Mookerjee was arrested by the Kashmir government because he had violated the 'permit' order. This is erroneous. There is, also, a suspicion in the minds of many about the conduct of the Government of India. The facts are as follows:

(i) On 8.5.53, Dr. Mookerjee before proceeding to Jammu & Kashmir "had intimated to Shri Sheikh Mohammad Abdullah by a telegram of his proposed visit and of the purpose of his visit, viz. to study conditions himself and to explore the possibilities of creating conditions leading to a peaceful settlement and to see, if possible, Hon'ble Shri Sheikh Mohammad Abdullah" [Appendix II-3]. A copy of this telegram was also sent to Mr. Nehru.

(ii) On 9.5.53, Sheikh Abdullah replied to the said telegram to the effect, "I am afraid your proposed visit to the State at the present juncture is inopportune and will not serve any useful purpose" (Appendix II-3).

(iii) The permit system had not been introduced by the Kashmir government, but by the Government of India, and the authorities of the Government of India not only did not prevent Dr. Mookerjee from entering Kashmir but the Deputy Commissioner of Gurdaspur on 11th May, 1953, under orders from the government, proceeded with him to the Madhopur check-post "to see that his entry into the state without permit was facilitated." Mr. Vaidya, a co-detenu, in his statement offered help to procure conveyance, etc. for us to go to Jammu. In fact, one of his subordinate officers took some of the persons of the party in his jeep up to Madhopur check-post. At Madhopur check-post, the District Magistrate and all his officers were standing and the District Magistrate wished us good journey.

(iv) Immediately thereafter, on the same day, as soon as he entered into Kashmir, the Superintendent of Police, Kathua (Jammu), who was ready with two orders, previously signed by the Chief Secretary and the Inspector-General of Police, Jammu & Kashmir, arrested him. The first order dated 10.5.53 directed Dr. Mookerjee not to enter, reside or remain in the state. The second order dated 11.5.53, which was also kept ready with the S.P. and was served within "not more than a minute" of the first one, was an order for arrest [Appendix-II-3]. Evidently, the alleged ground mentioned therein had no substance at all when the order was actually signed by the officer concerned, who was not even present at the time of arrest.

(v) The ground for arrest was not, as it could not be, his entry into the state without permit, but was that he "has acted, is acting and is about to act in a manner prejudicial to public safety and peace" and it was "in order to prevent him from so acting in the aforesaid manner". There was also a simultaneous order signed by the I.G. of Police, Kashmir, directing the Supdt., Central Jail, Srinagar, to "detain him in the Central Jail, Srinagar for a period of two months." The first two orders were purported to have been passed under Sections 3 & 4 of the Jammu & Kashmir Public Security Act, 2003 [Appendix II-3].

(vi) After Dr. Mookerjee's arrest, the Kashmir government passed an ordinance making it an offence for any one to enter the state without a state permit. But Dr. Mookerjee was not arrested under this ordinance. And yet Sh. Abdullah in his broadcast, after the arrest, declared that Dr. Mookerjee had been arrested for entering the state without a permit. Even after his death, Sh. Abdullah reiterated the same ground and said that even though "the permit system means some difficulty for us, we have to submit to the needs of the national security of India as defence of the country is paramount for every Indian" [Appendix I-E]. Thus, according to the Kashmir Premier, Dr. Mookerjee's arrest was for the 'national security' and 'defence' of India.

(vii) A criminal case for alleged violation of a prohibitory order was pending at Delhi against Dr. Mookerjee from before his arrest. It was expected that he would be allowed by the Kashmir government to come down to Delhi to stand his trial there. When, however, the Delhi trial magistrate wrote to the Chief Secretary, Jammu & Kashmir government, for sending down Dr. Mookerjee for recording his statement, the Kashmir government refused to concede to the request and replied that the time was too short and that steps could be taken if and when Dr. Mookerjee's presence was necessary at the trial. Meanwhile, the local government at Delhi (the prosecutors in that case) managed to delay the hearing on the ground of an alleged illness of a Sub-Inspector of Police, the last witness in the case. The magistrate, not being satisfied with the story, instituted personal enquiries into the matter and sent the witness for further medical examination by the local civil surgeon who, in his report, received in court on 2.6.53, stated that the Sub-Inspector had been kept under observation. The magistrate, by an order passed on the same day, observed that he had received an intimation from the Chief Secretary of Jammu & Kashmir government stating that Dr. Mookerjee was not likely to be produced in his court in the near future. The case was thus adjourned to 15th July, 1953, as Dr. Mookerjee's period of detention in Kashmir was reported to be fixed up to 13th July, 1953.

(viii) The statement of Sh. Abdullah immediately after Dr. Mookerjee's death, that "the government was considering to send him to Delhi immediately after

Shri Jawaharlal Nehru's return to India" is very significant [Appendix I-E].

(ix) In a written note left by Dr. Mookerjee, he refers to the "conspiracy between the Government of India and the Jammu & Kashmir government—the circumstances under which my entry was facilitated by Indian officials" [Appendix II-2]. In his letter dated 12th May, 1953, he wrote, "I was arrested yesterday though the Government of India did not prevent my coming without permit... Under peculiar circumstances, my stay in Srinagar has come to be arranged."

Thus, does the general suspicion find an echo in the remarks of Dr. Mookerjee himself?

II

EVENTS AFTER THE ARREST

Re: Statement of Pt. Shamlal Saraf, Minister for Health & Jails, Kashmir government: the only official version of the events [Appendix I-C]

The statement does not disclose that after the arrest of Dr. Mookerjee on the 11th May, he was taken in a jeep and, in spite of his protests, he was forced to travel till 2 a.m. in the morning through mountainous regions. The way in which he was rushed up to Srinagar, a distance of about 250 miles, with little rest, is described in Mr. Vaidya's statement [Appendix I-G1].

A

'Comforts' and 'Amenities' during Detention

(a) The sub-jail

The statement is full of praise for the 'picturesque villa' with all its amenities. Extracts have been quoted from Dr. Mookerjee's letters to establish that the "arrangements were to the satisfaction of Dr. Mookerjee". The version given is wrong as will appear from the facts stated hereunder.

It should be noted that the passages given at random from his letters dated 25th May and 4th June to his sister-in-law, though within inverted commas, are not exact quotations. Some lines—very important and relevant—have been left out. Some of those lines are quoted and referred to hereafter in their relevant contexts. It is also to be noted that Shri Tek Chand was a co-detenu, and not Dr. Mookerjee's 'private secretary'.

(i) The size of the bungalow with its compound was very small. There was not even accommodation for a fourth man and when Pandit Dogra arrived on the 19th June, one of the two co-detenus, in order to accommodate Pandit Dogra, had to shift to a tent, specially pitched outside the building.

(ii) There was not adequate space for walking. He was losing his appetite for want of exercise. His request for permission to have a stroll for an hour outside the compound was refused. The minister's statement that this was agreed to by the officers does not mention the date when it was so agreed.

As a matter of fact, Dr. Mookerjee had never received such permission. Mr. Vaidya's statement says that there was some verbal instruction to the police for allowing him to walk outside, but in the absence of a written order the police did not allow this [Appendix I-G1].

(iii) The villa had been converted into a 'sub-jail' as admitted by the government and as described in Col. Chopra's report.

Armed guards—10 to 12 in number—were on watch day and night.

(iv) There was only one lavatory—accessible through the room used by Dr. Mookerjee and this was used by the other two detenus also; so Dr. Mookerjee's room had to be used as a passage.

(v) The minister's statement says that the use of a telephone was arranged. This is misleading. It leaves the impression that the telephone could be used by Dr. Mookerjee. The fact is that the nearest telephone (as it appears from Mr. Vaidya's statement) was in the waterworks office building, some distance away from the sub-jail and being outside the compound, was not accessible to nor meant for the detenus. The telephone room also remained closed, except during office hours [Appendix I-G1].

(vi) The jeep was arranged for the Superintendent of the Jail to discharge his own duties and for his daily inspection and it was not an arrangement specially made for Dr. Mookerjee's convenience.

The following extracts from Dr. Mookerjee's letters speak for themselves:

Letter dated 18.5.53: "I am staying in a small bungalow... The bungalow is situated in a small but lovely garden... I walk on the narrow garden path... When you read this, you will feel how happy I must be. Alas, that is not possible. What physical comforts, what charms of nature, can bring you joy if your freedom is not yours... Send me a long reply full of news and stories—but not politics, of course! For, I am a prisoner here."

Letter dated 21.5.53 (in Bengali): "There are no means of going outside the small garden. There are armed guards watching day and night. I am completely cut off from the world outside. They have made a special jail for me... The natural scenery is very charming. Why should it not be so? But when one is imprisoned, there is no joy in such pleasures."

Letter dated 23.5.53: "It is a small bungalow within a well-kept fruit and flower garden... Of course, I am not allowed to go out of the compound—I have to walk on the narrow path of the small garden itself."

Letter dated 25.5.53 (in Bengali): "Permission is limited only to a walk along the garden path—it takes 2 or 3 minutes to cover the distance. It is there only and in the little open space that lies ahead of it that I take my stroll... This house is very small."

Letter dated 25.5.53 (in Bengali): "Permission could not

be had for a stroll outside the garden in the morning and in the afternoon. I take a walk in the narrow path inside the garden. The garden is not large... There are ten or twelve policemen who keep guard—lest there be loss of prestige!"

[Portions left out from the letter quoted in the minister's statement.]

Letter dated 31.5.53: "I am fairly well here—though without any exercise I am losing appetite..."

Letter dated 31.5.53 (in Bengali): "I am so so—but there is not much of movement—only walking inside the garden; it gives me no appetite."

Letter dated 3.6.53: "I am doing fairly well, except that owing to want of exercise, I have very little appetite..."

Letter dated 6.6.53 (in Bengali): "The pain in the right leg has again increased during the last two days. As it is, there is no scope even for a walk, except in the garden; and that gives me no appetite at all. If, on top of this, I have to be completely confined to bed or to sit still, it becomes still more unbearable for me."

Letter dated 15.6.53 (in Bengali): "I have very little appetite as I cannot take any walk" (received after his death).

(b) Food and other articles

It has been stated in the minister's statement that "Dr. Mookerjee made his own choice of food" and, according to the report of Col. Chopra dated 15.5.53 (apparently an official report as Inspector-General of Prisons) "the arrangements... with regard to the food are excellent and the quality of the food supplied cannot be improved upon." Again, on 9.6.53 his report was that "his feeding arrangements are in every way satisfactory" [Appendix I-C].

The letters already quoted above show how Dr. Mookerjee had been losing appetite and this continued till the last as evidenced by his letter dated 18.6.53 (which reached Calcutta after his death). He wrote, "I have little appetite and sometimes I have some difficulty in breathing..." It is also manifest that the food that was supplied to him was not the normal diet he used to take or best suited to his constitution.

How 'Alladin's lamp-like service' [Appendix I-C] was a fairy-tale with him will be amply proved by the fact that he had to ask for and get, from time to time, the following articles from his daughter in Delhi:

<table>
<tr><td>1.</td><td>A tin of biscuits</td><td>(referred to in his letters dated 12.5.53; 6.6.53)</td></tr>
<tr><td>2.</td><td>Nescafe</td><td>(referred to in letters dated 12.5.53 and 25.5.53)</td></tr>
<tr><td>3.</td><td>A muffler</td><td rowspan="2">(referred to in letters dated 21.5.53; 3.6.53)</td></tr>
<tr><td>4.</td><td>Mercolised wax</td></tr>
<tr><td>5.</td><td>A tin of Ovaltine</td><td rowspan="2">vide his letter dated 7.6.53</td></tr>
<tr><td>6.</td><td>A bottle of hair oil</td></tr>
<tr><td></td><td>Lemon drop lozenges</td><td rowspan="3">vide his letter dated 13.5.53</td></tr>
<tr><td></td><td>1 khata</td></tr>
<tr><td></td><td>1 writing pad</td></tr>
</table>

A prisoner in detention does not, for obvious reasons, ventilate his grievances or disclose his wants through censored letters. And of all persons Dr. Mookerjee would not, under any circumstances, have complained of his wants to anybody—not even to his near ones. He was fully conscious of the restrictions and hardships of a prisoner's life and faced them without grudge or grievance. Yet, there are indications in his letters to show the nature of life he was forced to live. Thus he had written in his letters:

Letter dated 4.6.53 (in Bengali): "Took also *bel* (sent from Calcutta). But where would I get the other ingredients for making sherbet?... The two attendants in the jail... serve me so well and are so very solicitous... why do 1 not drink milk... why do I take so little food—these are what they ask."

[Portions left out from his letter quoted in the minister's statement.]

Letter dated 6.6.53 (in Bengali): "I am indeed very cautious about my food. Boiled diet—vegetables. Fish is not available—they brought it only on two occasions... At 7 in the morning a cup of tea... A little before half past eight, I go to the garden and sit... There my meal is brought—2 cream cracker biscuits—Hasu (his daughter) has sent them—with a little butter, one half-boiled egg and a cup of milk-coffee... At 3.30, only tea—with lemon—and fruits (if any).... I take... the same menu both morning and evening. I take only one piece of bread. Boiled vegetables, meat occasionally and curd, both morning and evening. They brought me sweets only once or twice."

The diet taken by Dr. Mookerjee during the three days before his removal to the hospital is thus described by Mr. Vaidya:

"Two days previous to the last illness Dr. Mookerjee

had lost appetite and was taking very little food... Dr. Mookerjee took only tea, coffee and vegetable soup. On the 20th and 21st he took two cups of vegetable soup and one or two cups of tea and a cup of coffee in a day. He took a little orange juice also on the morning of 22nd on the advice of the doctor" [Appendix I-G1].

This was all the diet for a patient after he had been declared to be suffering from pleurisy.

(c) Irregularity in the dispatch and delivery, and disappearance of letters

In the life of a detenu, the importance of correspondence with the members of his family can never be denied. With Dr. Mookerjee the anxiety for home news was intense. Curiously enough, as his anxiety for his ailing daughter and mother became manifest—their letters were made scarce and at times they totally disappeared. The way in which his letters to and from the members of his family were being dealt with, will appear from the following extracts from his letters:

Letter dated 15.5.53: "I cannot write in Bengali as letters must pass through jail authorities and none can read Bengali. That is why I cannot write to mother and *Bowdi*. Ask them not to worry."

Letter dated 18.5.53: "Is this not funny that I have to write to you in English? I cannot write in Bengali as there is no one here who can censor it and pass it."

Letter dated 21.5.53 (in Bengali): 'There is a great deal of delay in the receipt and dispatch of letters, and also confusion. I do not know after how many days you will receive this letter."

Letter dated 29.5.53: "I wrote several letters to you, mother, *Bowdi* and *Antu*. Since your last telegram no letter has come from any of you."

Letter dated 31.5.53 (in Bengali): "The other day I was informed that I could write a few letters in Bengali. So I wrote to mother, you and *Bua*. I do not know what happened to those letters. A few days back, I got the information that the gentleman who censored Bengali letters was not here, so there would be delay in the dispatch of such letters."

Letter dated 31.5.53: "Express delivery makes no difference—except you pay-/2/ more!"

[This was written to his daughter who had, in her anxiety to help messages to reach him early, sent 'Express delivery' letters.]

Letter dated 4.6.53 (in Bengali): "Yesterday I was very happy to receive your letter written in Bengali. Before this, I did not receive any letter written in Bengali. I got a letter in English, typewritten. I have no idea what happened to the other letters... How did mother become so very ill? She must have become very weak. I have not received any letters from her since my arrival here. I have written 2 or 3 letters to her... After I had written this letter today, I got three of your letters—the delay has perhaps been due to the letters being written in Bengali."

Letter dated 7.6.53: "I was anxious not to have got your letter for some days. Today I got your letter of 1st June—which was posted on 1st and came here on 4th—and delivered to me today! You see how many days it takes for a letter to come from Delhi."

Letter dated 13.6.53: "Not received any letter from you or anyone else from home for the last 10 or 12 days. The last letter from Hasu was dated 30th May. Something is happening about the dak—I do not know where the letters are going... Just received your letter and *Bowdi's* letter of 4th June. The delay was due to the letters being written in Bengali—the Bengali censor is not easily available!"

Letter dated 13.6.53: "See I have to write in English—otherwise there will be delay in censoring! I got your letter of 3rd June only today! You must have got my previous letters. For the last ten days, no letter came from any of you, nor from Hasu."

Letter dated 14-6.53: "Glad to get your letter day before yesterday after a long time. *Thakurma's* letter was in Bengali; it took a longer time. Hence I am replying to you in English! Today I have posted in a separate cover letters in Bengali to *Thakurma, Jathaima, Sejka, Bulbul*—I do not know when they will get them. Hasu's letters this month have become very irregular. Her last letter was dated 30th May. I wrote to her four letters and sent one telegram—but no reply. I do not know what is happening... I hope you will get this soon."

[His youngest son got this at Calcutta on 26th June, four days after his death! The other letters referred to were posted at Srinagar by the Kashmir authorities on the 24th June and reached Calcutta on the 27th June.]

Letters dated 15.6.53: [These letters, along with two others, were despatched by the government of Kashmir on 24.6.53—one day after sending his dead body—and were received at Calcutta on 27.6.53. The packet in which these were sent also brought back to Calcutta letters, written by his mother and sister-in-law, which had reached Srinagar on 11.6.53 and 16.6.53, but had never been delivered to Dr. Mookerjee.]

To his sister-in-law (in Bengali): "I do not know after how many days you will get it. When the magistrate came on Friday, I asked him why there was so much delay in receiving and despatching letters written in Bengali. He told me that the gentleman who translates all these letters is not always available here. I do not know who he is. I told him if he could trust me I could myself translate these letters and send them to the magistrate, then there would not be so much delay. I do not know whether he will agree to this. Hasu, however, writes in English; I also do the same. But since the beginning of June I have written to her four letters and her last letter which was dated the 30th May I got here on the 6th June. I do not understand all this. Anyway, it is no use worrying; such things will happen. Only I am worried when I do not get any news of you. How is mother? I got her letter along with Antu's day before yesterday. She has, of course, written she is well though gradually feeling weaker, but she has also expressed her apprehension that she would not see me again. I felt very sad when I read this. Has her condition much worsened? I, of course, cannot do anything from here... I shall be very far away on the 6th of July. Isn't it?" (6th July was his birthday)

To mother (in Bengali): "I was delighted to receive your letter after such a long time. Letters written in Bengali take a long time to reach—that is why your letter took such a long time in coming. I am well—do not be worried about me. Why have you written that we two would not meet again? Meet we must, and then I am sure I shall see you in better health. I do often think of you. Take good care of your health, whenever you feel unwell. *Pranams* to you. Please write to me again."

[And her letter was already there, held back by the Kashmir authorities—never to be delivered during his life-time and was returned after his death to her along with his above letter!]

The post marks on the letters also show the inordinate delay in delivering letters even after they had reached Srinagar.

(d) Interview with friends and relations

Though the Kashmir minister's statement does not anywhere refer to any facilities given to Dr. Mookerjee for interviews with friends and relations, Maulana Azad in his statement dated 23rd June said that the government of Jammu & Kashmir transferred him to a 'nursing home' and "arranged that his friends present in Srinagar should be by his side" [Appendix I-D].

But, the facts are as follows:

(i) Dr. Mookerjee's eldest son made an attempt to proceed to Kashmir and interview his father, but having failed to immediately get the necessary permit sent the following wire to Dr. Mookerjee on 11.6.53:

"Kashmir permit not immediately available."

(ii) Some relations of Dr. Mookerjee happened to be at Srinagar during his detention. They also tried to get permission for interview but failed.

(iii) When Dr. Mookerjee was being removed to the hospital, his two co-detenus wanted to accompany him and stay with him in the hospital but this was refused.

(iv) According to the Kashmir government communique [Appendix I-B] Dr. Mookerjee, at 11 p.m. on the 22nd June, began to be restless and oxygen had to be given. It appears from Mr. Vaidya's statement that Dr. Mookerjee, at about 1 a.m. (when he must have realised that his condition was critical), had pressed for the presence of his companions by his side. But no attempt was made by the authorities to secure their presence even during those last hours [Appendix I-G1]. Maulana Azad's statement that the government had arranged for the presence of Dr. Mookerjee's friends by his side is without any foundation.

(v) It should be noted that Mr. Trivedi, the counsel, could get the facility for interview only after the High Court of Kashmir had intervened.

B

His Illness

It is significant to note that the Kashmir government seems to have been aware of the 'weak state of health' of

Dr. Mookerjee. This was admitted by Sheikh Abdullah himself on 25.6.53 when he said that though technically Dr. Mookerjee was under detention, "the government had allowed him all facilities particularly in view of his weak state of health" [Appendix 1-E]. The theory of 'technical detention' and the story of allowing all facilities to him can be examined in the light of the facts already disclosed. How he was treated during his different periods of illness in detention will appear from the following facts:

[It is to be noted that Col. Chopra's report on 15th May (quoted in the Health Minister's statement) [Appendix I-C] was on a visit three days after Dr. Mookerjee's arrival at the sub-jail.]

(i) Pain in the right leg. The minister's statement says: "On may 18, Dr. Mookerjee complained of pain in the right leg in the right calf. It was accompanied by slight swelling and varicose veins were observed. The pain disappeared within two days under rest and treatment but as a precautionary measure, aftercare was continued for about a week more. Again on June 5th he had a slight pain of the aching type in the right calf, without any temperature and swelling. He was seen by Dr. Ali Mohammed accompanied by Dr. Prem Nath Dhar, house surgeon of the state hospital, the same day. The past history of osteoarthritis and probably also of gout was taken into consideration and treatment given accordingly. He recovered within a couple of days" [Appendix I-C].

But, this is what Dr. Mookerjee says in his letters:

Letter dated 10.5.53: "I have a nasty pain in my right leg—doctor has asked me to take to bed completely."

Letter dated 21.5.53 (in Bengali): "I had to be confined

to bed for a few days with a pain in the right leg. I do not know why I had this acute pain. The doctor is attending every day. He has prescribed medicine to be taken by mouth and for application. He said this was due to cold. There was slight fever. I am well today and can walk."

Letter dated 25.5.53 (in Bengali): "I suffered for some days from a sudden pain in the right leg. The doctor attended every day. I am now well. Perhaps it was due to cold."

Letter dated 25.5.53 (in Bengali): "For some days I was absolutely confined to bed all the time owing to a pain in the right leg. The pain has decreased since day before yesterday. I can walk just a little inside the garden" [portions left out from the letter in the minister's statement].

It is interesting to note that when Dr. Mookerjee was writing about his illness in these letters, Pandit Nehru on 23rd and 24th May was at Srinagar 'for rest' accompanied by Dr. Katju, the Home Minister, and in his letter to Dr. Mookerjee's mother, Mr. Nehru says: "when I went to Kashmir... I enquired particularly... about his health... I found... that he was keeping well. I was happy to leam this at the time" [Appendix I-K].

Letter dated 4.6.33 (in Bengali): "I am so so: the pain in the right leg had decreased, but has come back again since yesterday—it starts from just below the knee. It is difficult to walk. I am applying hot water bag. For some days, I am having breathing difficulties. I do not know why..." [portions left out from the letter quoted in the minister's statement]

Letter dated 6.6.53 (in Bengali): "I was on the whole keeping well but the pain in the right leg has again increased during the last two days—I do not know why this is happening. The doctor came yesterday and prescribed medicine. He said I should not stand up at all during the whole day. As it is, there is no scope even for a walk except in the garden and that gives me no appetite at all. If on top of this, I have to be completely confined to bed or to sit still, it becomes still more unbearable for me. Moreover, for some days I have been running a temperature in the evenings—not much; 99°. There is burning sensation in the eyes and face. I am taking medicine."

Immediately after the receipt of this letter, on or about 12.6.53, Dr. Mookerjee's brother saw Dr. Bidhan Chandra Roy and apprised him of Dr. Mookerjee's ill health and requested him to contact Kashmir. Dr. Roy expressed his anxiety and said that he would get in touch with Sheikh Abdullah. Dr. Mookerjee's son, also made an attempt at Delhi to secure a permit to proceed to Kashmir, but in vain. In his letter dated 13.6.53, Dr. Mookerjee, however, wrote: "I am keeping fairly well."

Letter dated 18.6.53: "I am doing fairly well now, except I have little appetite and sometimes I have some difficulty in breathing. For some days I had slow fever in the evening and a nasty pain in the right leg. All that is gone now... "

[Addressed to his daughter at Poona; received at Calcutta after death.]

Letter dated 21.6.53: "I have not been well for the last 3 or 4 days."

[Received after death: the signature and the writing not normal].

From the above letters it will be observed that:

(a) The pain had appeared some time before the 18th May, that is, within a week of his arrival. According to Mr. Vaidya's statement, "Three days after our arrival there, Dr. Mookerjee fell ill of pain in the right leg and he had temperature. We had no thermometer... The doctor came the next day" [Appendix I-G1].

(b) It did not disappear within 'two days' but continued for some time.

(c) The pain was accompanied by fever.

(d) The pain was acute and kept him absolutely confined to bed for some days.

(e) The report of the recurrence of "a slight pain of the aching type without any temperature" on the 5th June and his recovery within a "couple of days" is incorrect. The previous pain had only decreased and it intensified from 3rd June and continued for some days. Even Col. Chopra's report dated 9th June, as quoted in the Health Minister's statement, admits that there was still some pain on that date [Appendix I-C].

(f) "Without any temperature" is not correct. He had been getting 'slow fever' in the evenings.

(g) Even though the pain reappeared with intensity on 3rd June, medical attendance, according to Col. Chopra's report, was made available on 5th June, that is, after two days.

(h) It was not a “slight pain of the aching type” but a ‘nasty pain’.

(i) The pain, according to the first attending physician, was due to ‘cold’. The ‘gout history’ was a subsequent discovery. Dr. Mookerjee had never before in his life an attack of pain of that nature and in that particular region of his leg. It was apparently a symptom of a new malady.

Col. Chopra’s subsequent report for the period from 9th June to 23rd June (quoted in the minister’s statement—Appendix I-C).

Perfect health up to 19th June

This report, it is apparent, was submitted by the Inspector-General of Prisons after Dr. Mookerjee’s death. Col. Chopra does not appear to have himself visited Dr. Mookerjee after 9th June. He went to the Hospital ‘a few minutes too late’ after Dr. Mookerjee’s death. The report about ‘perfect health upto 19th June’ is apparently based on two grounds; firstly, Dr. Mookerjee had not complained of any ailment to the Superintendent of Jail on the 19th June and secondly, Sardar Hukum Singh, MP (who is not a physician and who had in his presidential address at the State Akali Conference, described the Parishad agitation as ‘extremely harmful’) found Dr. Mookerjee on the 16th June ‘quite alright’.

It may be recalled that Col. Chopra in his previous report dated 9th June had said that Dr. Mookerjee had still some pain on 9th June. It is not known when that pain disappeared, if at all, but it is clearly admitted in the report that Dr. Mookerjee was not examined by any doctor after 5th June.

His letter dated 18.6.53 (received in Calcutta long after his death): "I am doing fairly well now, except I have little appetite and sometimes I have some difficulty in breathing. For some days I had slow fever in the evening and a nasty pain in the right leg. All that is gone now."

Letter dated 21.6.53 [received after death—not written to any member of the family]: "I have not been well for the last 3 or 4 days."

The story of 'perfect health upto 19th June' is thus a myth. There was in fact no medical treatment or attendance or any examination during this period, though he was ill and sometimes having 'difficulty in breathing'.

Illness from 20th to 22nd June

The minister's statement tries to minimise a serious illness by use of expressions like 'indisposition', 'slight pain', etc.

The temperature on the 20th June is said to be 99.2° only in the report. But the facts were otherwise. A temperature chart [Appendix II-i] kept by Dr. Mookerjee himself in his own handwriting during those three days has been found in his briefcase, which he had left behind, locked up, in the sub-jail. It runs as follows:

20/6

8 a.m.	99.4°
12 noon	99.2°
4 p.m.	101.2°
8 p.m.	100.2°

21/6

8 a.m.	99°
11.30 a.m.	98.4°
4 p.m.	100°
8 p.m.	100°

At about four a.m.—heart pain, heavy perspiration, sinking feeling—temperature suddenly dropped. Temperature taken at

5.30 a.m.—97°

7.00 a.m.—98°

8.00 a.m.—98.2°

Immediately after the death, this illness was described by Maulana Azad on 23.6.53 in the following terms: "He caught a chill three days ago which developed into dry pleurisy". Mr. Nehru's version was that 'he felt somewhat unwell on the 22nd'.

The events as they happened from the 20th to the 23rd June and as they appeared to Mr. Vaidya. a co-detenu, are described in his statement [Appendix I-G1]. Mr. Trivedi, Dr. Mookerjee's counsel, has also issued a statement based on his own knowledge [Appendix I-G2]. The following salient facts emerge out of the facts already stated and also from the aforesaid two statements vis-a-vis the government versions:

1. Dr. Mookerjee was ill even before the 20th June.
2. He had complained of 'breathing difficulties' in his letters dated 4th June and 18th June. Apparently the doctors had taken no notice of the fact, nor adopted any precautionary measures whatsoever.

3. His illness as diagnosed by Dr. Ali Mohammad in the morning of 20th June was 'dry pleurisy'. Whether there can be a sudden onset of dry pleurisy without any premonitory symptoms or indications is a matter to be judged by experts.
4. Maulana Azad's statement that he 'caught a chill' on the 20th June which developed into dry pleurisy is contradicted by the Kashmir minister's statement itself.
5. The minister's statement [Appendix I-C] says that the jail authorities received a telephone message on June 20th that Dr. Mookerjee was indisposed and immediately Dr. Amar Nath Raina (Medical Officer-in-Charge, jail dispensary) and Dr. Ali Mohammad went to see him. Dr. Mookerjee, it is said, complained of 'slight pain'. On the other hand, Mr. Vaidya says that the pain with 'high temperature' started in the night between the 19th and 20th June and the pain was 'acute'. The doctors arrived at about 11.30 a.m.
6. The version given in the official report that his condition improved and he felt much better afterwards is contradicted by the temperature chart in Dr. Mookerjee's own handwriting. The temperature shot up to 101.2° in the afternoon of 20th June.
7. Even though the doctors arrived at 11.30 a.m. on the 20th medicines were not made available before 3.30 p.m.

8. The streptomycin injection was given in spite of Dr. Mookerjee's protests that he had been advised by his family physician not to take it as it did not suit his system.
9. The injection was given by the jail doctor.
10. The two records of the previous history of his illness in 1937 and 1944, as alleged to have been given by Dr. Mookerjee to the doctors on the 20th and 22nd June, are inconsistent.
11. Mr. Vaidya says that on 20th June "Dr. Mookerjee told the superintendent that news of his illness should be sent to his relatives" [Appendix I-G1]. But no such intimation was sent nor any bulletin issued by the government.
12. On the 21st June except for the jail doctor (qualifications not known) no other doctor, not even Dr. Ali Mohammed, had visited or examined him. The jail doctor saw him at about 10 a.m. His temperature rose and the pain increased from the afternoon, but there was no medical attendance.
13. Even though pleurisy had been declared in the morning of 20th June, no nursing arrangements were made between 20th and 22nd June at the sub-jail.
14. The diet taken during 20th and 21st June was as follows:
    Two cups of vegetable soup
    one or two cups of tea and
    a cup of coffee in course of a whole day.

15. On 22nd June, Dr. Mookerjee thus recorded [Appendix II-i] his condition at about 4 a.m.: "Heart pain, heavy perspiration, sinking feeling; temperature suddenly dropped. Temperature taken at 5.30 a.m.—97°" (in the mouth), even when (according to Mr. Vaidya) perspiration had stopped. Medical attendance could be requisitioned over the phone only between 5.15 and 5.30 and the doctors arrived at about 7.30 a.m.

16. No laboratory tests or pathological examinations were made so long as Dr. Mookerjee was in the sub-jail. No X-ray had been taken in the sub-jail or the hospital, but there was merely a proposal for taking it in the morning of the 23rd June at 9 a.m.

17. In spite of insistence on the part of the co-detenus, none of them was permitted to accompany Dr. Mookerjee to the hospital. Even the two jail attendants who had been attending on him during detention were not allowed to go with him.

18. In spite of the diagnosis of heart attack of coronary type, his family was not informed.

19. That Dr. Mookerjee had been in a weak state of health throughout his detention and that the Kashmir government was aware of the fact, was admitted by Sheikh Abdullah himself on 25.6.53 [Appendix I-E].

20. Dr. Mookerjee was removed to the hospital not in a 'comfortable car' as stated in the minister's statement, but in a very small car in which he could only sit in a most uncomfortable position.

Further, the hospital was about 10 miles away from the sub-jail. The most staggering fact is that a patient suffering from coronary trouble was taken in such a car under such conditions for such a long distance.

21. Dr. Mookerjee was not kept in any nursing home but in the gynaecological ward of the state hospital.

22. Even at the hospital, he was kept as a prisoner under police guard.

23. No attempt was made to secure the presence of his co-detenus or of Mr. Trivedi to be by his side when Dr. Mookerjee's condition became critical and he had pressed for their presence.

24. It is most curious that Dr. Mookerjee, who had been all along so anxious for home news and writing letters so often, does not seem to have written any letter to the members of his family at Calcutta after 15th June. His letters of 15th June reached Calcutta on the 27th June. But what happened to the letters which he must have written to them after 15th June?

25. The careless manner in which arrangements for medical attendance had been made even in the hospital is illustrated by one striking fact. Even a cursory examination of the Kashmir government communique and the minister's statement will show that on the night of 22.6.53, Dr. Mookerjee had been left in the sole charge of one, Dr. Jagannath Zutshi (qualifications not known, but described as the house surgeon of the hospital). He had seen

Dr. Mookerjee for the first time at the hospital at 11 a.m. on 22.6.53, and yet it was this doctor alone who seems to have attended to Dr. Mookerjee on that fateful night and none of the two doctors (Dr. A.H. Mohammad and Dr. Ramnath Parhar) who were supposed to have previously examined the patient and diagnosed his illness, was present during those critical hours or at the time of Dr. Mookerjee's death.

A report about the events after Dr. Mookerjee's arrest was published in the *Organiser*, dated 20th July, 1953 [Appendix 1-L].

C

Diagnosis and Medical Treatment

The question of diagnosis of Dr. Mookerjee's illness, the medical treatment given to him, the arrangements for his diet and nursing, the taking of precautionary and emergency measures, proper handling and examination of the patient, have not been directly dealt with in this review. A number of leading members of the medical profession have given their views on the matter and some of them have been printed in Appendix I-H. Their opinion is that there was, to say the least, gross negligence on the part of the government and the doctors in charge.

D

Dr. Mookerjee's Last Telegram

Much prominence and importance have been given by the government to the last telegram sent by Dr. Mookerjee on 22nd June from the hospital to his family. It has been suggested in the Health Minister's statement [Appendix I-C] that the telegram shows that (i) Dr. Mookerjee was doing better and (ii) he was being treated well. It further states that the government wanted to send a message, but Dr. Mookerjee said that he himself would send it, and he gave it at 2 p.m.

As against this, the following relevant facts are to be borne in mind:

(i) Dr. Mookerjee's statement in the telegram that he was better and that there were satisfactory medical arrangements should be taken in the light of the conditions and circumstances prevailing around him. He was in detention. He knew that his message would be censored. The message was meant for the members of his family, particularly, his mother, who were all far away from him. Above all, it should be remembered that on 20th June, immediately after he had been declared to be suffering from pleurisy, he had asked the Superintendent to send intimation of his illness to his family. He must have known that it was not done on 20th nor on 21st June. No wonder, therefore, that on 22nd June after having been removed to the hospital, when he was asked whether he would like any information of his removal to be sent to his relatives, he should say that "he would prefer to inform them himself".

(ii) The telegram shows that he had been suffering from pleurisy for the last three days, which suggests that no information was or could be sent on all those days.

(iii) The telegram did not refer to Dr. Mookerjee's heart attack, even though the diagnosis had been made at noon on that date.

(iv) After all, a patient can never be expected to be the best judge either of his own condition or of the appropriateness and adequacy of the treatment.

(v) It is a curious coincidence that the only message, apparently released by the Kashmir government about Dr. Mookerjee's illness and published in the papers after his death [Appendix I-A], was couched almost in the same language as Dr. Mookerjee's telegram and it also did not disclose that he had a coronary attack.

(vi) Even this telegram of Dr. Mookerjee, which is said in the statement to have been handed over by him at about 2 p.m., was delayed at Srinagar till 5 p.m. and was despatched thereafter with the result that the telegram reached Calcutta on 23rd June, some time after the news of his death had been received.

III

INFORMATION OF DEATH RECEIVED IN CALCUTTA

It was the morning of 23rd June, 1953. At about 5.45 a.m. the telephone rang at 77 Asutosh Mookerjee

Road, Calcutta, the residence of Dr. Mookerjee. The operator informed that there was a personal trunk call from Srinagar for Justice Mookerjee (eldest brother of Dr. Mookerjee). The news immediately went round the house and all the members of the family gathered round the phone, expecting to hear the voice of Dr. Mookerjee. His mother was helped near the machine so that she might talk to her son directly. As Justice Mookerjee was trying to get the connection through, all waited with eager expectation. Justice Mookerjee failed to catch the voice at the Kashmir end. The Delhi operator, who had put the line through, intervened and helped to relay the message. The operator's voice could be heard as directly talking to Kashmir, but the Kashmir voice was off the line. The Delhi operator was getting the message from Srinagar and repeating it to Justice Mookerjee: "Srinagar tells me that there is a message from Sheikh Abdullah to you and the message is that Dr. Syama Prasad Mookerjee is dead and Sheikh Abdullah wants to know 'what about the disposal of the body?'" Justice Mookerjee, stunned at the news, told the operator that he could not understand anything and wanted to know what had actually happened and who the informant was. At this the operator told Srinagar that Justice Mookerjee wanted further information and then said to Justice Mookerjee, "Srinagar says that Dr. Mookerjee had an attack of pleurisy three days back and was yesterday removed to hospital where he had a sudden heart attack and expired at 3.40 a.m." As Justice Mookerjee could not believe the information, he insisted on knowing who the informant was. Thereupon the operator, after again speaking to Srinagar, informed him that Mr. Dhar, the Deputy Home Minister, was on the line. Justice Mookerjee immediately replied that the body must be sent to Calcutta and he demanded full information. The operator, after a talk with Srinagar, told Justice Mookerjee that the Kashmir authorities would ring him up after half an hour.

Thus came the news of his end to his mother and other members of his family.

Mr. Nehru, however, in his letter to Shri Atulya Ghosh, wrote the following account:

"You refer to the way news was communicated to Justice Mookerjee by telephone. As a matter of fact it took a long time to get the telephone connection. After this was obtained, it was impossible to talk directly as nothing could be heard. The minister who was on the line in Srinagar, Durga Prasad Dhar, ultimately had to ask the Delhi operator to give the message to the Calcutta operator, who repeated it to Justice Mookerjee. You can well imagine what happened to the message in the course of this double relay. It must have been distorted and only the briefest message was given. I have had a talk with Durga Prasad Dhar, who says that he gave a long message, but naturally only a distorted form went through" (Appendix I-J).

This is not correct.

It is further to be observed that the *Amrita Bazar Patrika* in its issue of 24th June contains the following:

"A flash message from Kashmir government conveying the melancholy news reached the Government of India. Union Home Secretary A.V. Pai has instructed the Kashmir government to get in touch with relatives of Dr. Mookerjee about funeral arrangements."

This shows that the Kashmir government informed Mr. Pai in the first instance and it was only on the instruction of Mr. Pai that the Kashmir government sent the message to Dr. Mookerjee's family. The Kashmir government did not think that the message should be conveyed to the family at the earliest possible moment. The story about difficulty in getting telephone connection does not explain this. It is also not correct that the Calcutta operator relayed the message to Justice Mookerjee. It was the Delhi operator (at times speaking in Hindi), who relayed the message to Justice Mookerjee and, while relaying, the operator was in direct touch with Srinagar.

Subsequent events during that day, 23rd June, may be briefly told. At about 11 a.m. Bakshi Ghulam Mohammed phoned to say that the plane with Dr. Mookerjee's body took off from Srinagar at 10.30 a.m. and was expected to reach Calcutta at about 3 p.m. The plane, however, reached Dum Dum at 9 p.m. Mr. Trivedi, who came with the body, mentions in his statement [Appendix I-G2] some reasons for this inordinate delay. An enquiry, if made, will reveal what part was played by the Government of India in the matter and whether the India government had deliberately caused this delay so that the body might not reach Calcutta before nightfall.

IV

DR. MOOKERJEE'S DIARY AND MANUSCRIPT/WRITINGS

More light would certainly be thrown on the tragedy if Dr. Mookerjee's diary and other writings were available for scrutiny.

Dr. Mookerjee in his letters had repeatedly mentioned that he had been spending his time in detention in reading and writing. He also used to write his diary regularly and his fellow detenus testify that he kept up the habit in the-sub-jail. When Dr. Mookerjee was removed to the hospital he must have taken his diary, if not his other writings, with him. The diary and these writings were not sent back by the Kashmir government to his family with his other belongings. Dr. Mookerjee's brother requested the Kashmir authorities to return them but they totally denied their possession thereof [Appendix I-K]. There is naturally a strong suspicion that these writings, and particularly the diary, have been deliberately withheld All possible steps should be taken for the recovery of these valuable documents.

Such are the facts so far revealed from most authentic sources, and they are here placed before the people of India so that they might see through the desperate effort made by Messrs. Nehru and Abdullah to ring down a hasty curtain over so tragic an end.

□

Appendix-I

A

AMRITA BAZAR PATRIKA, DATED 23RD JUNE, 1953

(From Our Special Representative)

Srinagar, June 22

Dr. Syama Prasad Mookerjee, now in detention here, was today admitted in government nursing home following an attack of pleurisy. Government doctors are now attending on him.

An official spokesman said Dr. Mookerjee's condition was not serious and that he was receiving the best medical attention.

B

KASHMIR GOVERNMENT COMMUNIQUE, DATED 23RD JUNE, 1953 PHYSICIANS' REPORT

Srinagar, June 23: The two doctors attending on Dr. Syama Prasad Mookerjee, Dr. Ali Mohammad, M.R.C.P. *[Edin.)* and Dr. Ramnath Parhar, M.D. *(Edin.),* issued the following report, according to a press communique issued by the Jammu & Kashmir government:

"Dr. Mookerjee had an attack of pain lasting two minutes in chest over the heart area on the morning of 22nd June, 1953. The pain was accompanied by perspiration and a feeling of general weakness. There was fall of blood pressure, a constant feeling of heaviness in the chest and a feeling of lack of energy. He was seen at his detention camp at Nishat Bagh at 7 a.m. by medical officer (Jail) and Dr. Ali Mohammad, physician, state hospital. After restorative measures were given on the spot, his condition improved and arrangements were made for his removal to the nursing home of the state hospital, where he was admitted at 12 noon. Blood, urine and electrocardiographic investigations were carried out and a provisional diagnosis of heart attack (coronary type) was made and treatment started with sedatives. Antibiotics were given and oxygen administered as necessary. His condition improved and he was cheerful. The physicians attending were Dr. Ali Mohammad, M.R.C.P. *{Edin.)* and Dr. Ramnath Parhar, M.D. *(Edin.)*.

At 7-30 p.m. he was seen by the District Magistrate and Shri Trivedi, his counsel, to whom he dictated some notes and signed some cheques.

At 9 p.m. his general condition was fairly good except for low blood pressure and rapid pulse.

At 11 p.m. oxygen was given to allay restlessness which started at that time, his blood pressure fell to 100/80. Glucose with aminophylline was given intravenously.

At 1 a.m. he got pain in the heart area and became restless. Pulse was feeble and blood pressure 90/70.

Oxygen was continued. To relieve pain, pethidine, one c.c., was given.

At 2.30 a.m. his condition was as above. Respiration and pulse became imperceptible, coramine and aminophylline were given intravenously.

At 3 a.m., condition was as above. Pulse was slightly perceptible. Oxygen was continued with intravenous coramine given again.

At 3.20 a.m. pulse was again imperceptible. Respiration feeble and irregular. Oxygen was continued.

At 3.40 a.m. respiration and pulse stopped.

—UPI

C

STATEMENT OF PT. S.L. SARAF, MINISTER FOR HEALTH & JAILS, KASHMIR, DATED 1.7.53

The circumstances leading to the tragic demise of Dr. Syama Prasad Mookerjee have already been explained in a press communique issued by the Jammu & Kashmir government on June 23rd. Some details of the illness and the treatment administered at various stages were given in the medical report quoted in the communique.

I observe that there is an understandable desire on the part of some of our countrymen to have fuller information about the sad and untimely death of a national figure. I appreciate their anxiety. We spared no efforts to save the precious life of Dr. Mookerjee. That these efforts should have failed has caused us as much sorrow as to our other countrymen.

Dr. Mookerjee was arrested on 11th May, 1953 along with Shri Guru Dutt Vaidya and Shri Tek Chand Sharma. They reached Srinagar on the following day and were put up in a private bungalow above the Nishat Garden, known as 'Heather Villa'.

Commanding a full view of the Dal Lake and its surroundings, 'Heather Villa' has a garden and an orchard attached to it. The villa is well furnished and has modern sanitary fittings. For the convenience of Dr. Mookerjee and his companions, the use of a telephone in the vicinity of the villa was arranged. The extent to which these arrangements were to the satisfaction of Dr. Mookerjee and his colleagues may be judged from the following extracts from their letters.

Writing to his sister-in-law on 25th May, 1953, Dr. Mookerjee said:

"... The house and the garden are situated at the foot of a mountain. The road runs right below the garden. After that the land moves up again to the mountains. Again there is a Dal Lake which I can see clearly both from the house and garden. The garden is full of fruit and flowering trees. Strawberries and cherries are now in full bloom... a stream runs through the garden... The Jail Superintendent comes every afternoon with kitchen provisions and my mail and papers. The milk here is very good; I drink it every morning. The butter is good and fresh... I spend my time in reading books and in writing down my thoughts."

In the course of another letter to his sister-in-law, on 4th June, 1953, Dr. Mookerjee wrote:

"Two employees of the jail do our cooking, washing, cleaning, making beds and serving the food. They are both very nice persons. They look after me so solicitously that I am often amazed."

Again on 4th June 1953, he wrote to Shri S.C. Banerjee in London:

"... the authorities are taking all care to meet my physical comforts. My health is fairly all right except I had a bad pain in the right leg for one week due to cold perhaps."

On 2nd June, 1953 Shri N.C. Chatterjee wrote to Dr. Mookerjee in Srinagar: "I am glad to know that the Kashmir government has been treating you properly."

Dr. Mookerjee's private secretary, Shri Tek Chand Sharma, who was with him in the camp, wrote to Shri Mahesh Chandra Sharma at Dehra Dun, "Everything is well here. We are all happy... we have no difficulties whatsoever."

Again on 15th May Shri Sharma wrote: "Over here we are all well and are spending a peaceful time... the food is good and the living comfortable... we have only to ask for a thing, as if 'Alladin's lamp' is at our disposal. The days are spent in eating, reading, writing and conversation. Every day we get the *Hindustan Times, Hindustan Standard* and *Tej* from Delhi by air which give us all the news."

On 5th June, 1953 Shri Tek Chand wrote to Shri Bhupal Singh Gupta of Delhi: "... and so in this state of mind we are enjoying a fine, long picnic. It is really an exciting and stirring sensation to be enjoying all the lovely beauty of Kashmir in this capacity.

"Well, we are all happy and in good health. Doctor Sahib is slightly indisposed today. There is a little pain in his right leg but there is nothing serious to be worried about..."

On the day of his arrival, Dr. Mookerjee was examined

by Dr. Ali Mohammad, M.R.C.P. (*Edin.*), physician specialist of the state hospital.

Dr. Mookerjee made his own choice of food. The Superintendent of Jail, Shri Srikanth, an officer with long experience, was personally made responsible to look after the comforts and amenities in Dr. Mookerjee's camp, and a jeep was specially provided for the purpose.

He and his colleagues were provided with newspapers, books and articles of stationery and arrangements were made to carry mail to and from the camp every day.

They moved about freely in the garden. Later on, in response to his desire, as conveyed through Sardar Hukam Singh, M.P. and Col. Sir Ram Nath Chopra, Director of Health Services and Inspector-General of Prisons, it was agreed that Dr. Mookerjee, if he so liked, may be permitted to have longer walks outside the premises of the garden.

On 15th May, 1953, Col. Chopra inspected the camp and sent the following report to the Minister of Health:

"Accompanied by the Superintendent of Jail, Srinagar, I inspected the sub-jail which is at present housed in a small rented house. The house is situated in a beautiful garden with excellent outlook and view. The house has ample furniture for the comforts of the detenus. The accommodation is sufficient for the three detenus who are housed there at present. The arrangements made by the Superintendent of Jail with regard to their food are excellent and the quality of the food supplies cannot be improved upon.

"The health of the three detenus is good. Dr. Syama Prasad Mookerjee is in good health and desires:

1. That he may be allowed to have longer walks (outside the premises of the garden);
2. That (more) literature in the form of journals and books may be supplied to him:
3. He said that he was anxious about his daughter who was recovering from tuberculosis of lungs. She had returned from Switzerland after treatment and was at present in Delhi in a very warm climate quite unsuitable for her condition.

"Dr. Mookerjee said that as he was not sure how long he would have to stay here, he was anxious that his daughter should get away from Delhi and should come up to Kashmir, provided arrangements could be made to give her treatment of lung collapse by injecting air twice a month which she was receiving. I said that there would be no difficulty about this and our tuberculosis specialist would attend to her and do the needful."

The request for journals and books was complied with immediately. Besides, the detenus were allowed to get books and journals from their friends also.

On 19th May, Dr. Mookerjee complained of pain in the right leg in the right calf. It was accompanied by slight swelling and varicose veins were observed. The pain disappeared within two days under rest and treatment but as a precautionary measure, aftercare was continued for about a week more.

Again on 5th June he had a slight pain of the aching type in the right calf without any temperature and swelling. He was seen by Dr. Ali Mohammad, accompanied by Dr.

Prem Nath Dhar, house surgeon of the state hospital, the same day. The past history of osteoarthritis and probably of gout was taken into consideration and treatment given accordingly. He recovered within a couple of days.

On 9th June, Col. Sir Ram Nath Chopra again visited the camp and, sent the following report:

"Today I found Dr. Mookerjee quite cheerful and fit although there is still some pain in the leg. He is being looked after very well and his feeding arrangements are in every way satisfactory. He is being supplied plenty of reading material, papers, etc. to keep him occupied."

The period between 9th June and the date of Dr. Mookerjee's demise, 3.40 a.m., 23rd June, is covered by a subsequent report received from Col. Sir Ram Nath Chopra which says:

"He remained in perfect health up to 19th June. The Superintendent of Jail, Pt. Shrikanth was with him on the said date up to 6.00 p.m. and Dr. Mookerjee had no complaint of any ailment to make."

On 16th June, 1953, Sardar Hukam Singh, MP met Dr. Mookerjee and, as has been publicly stated by him, found the latter 'quite all right'.

Sardar Hukam Singh, it may be stated, had met Dr. Mookerjee in an attempt to find ways and means of ending the Praja Parishad agitation in Jammu. Subsequently, he met Sheikh Sahib and conveyed to him Dr. Mookerjee's suggestion for facilities for a meeting with Pt. Prem Nath Dogra. Accordingly Pandit Dogra was brought to Srinagar on 19th June, 1953 and put up with Dr. Mookerjee.

On 20th June, the jail authorities received a telephone

message that Dr. Mookerjee was indisposed. The medical officer in charge, jail dispensary. Pt. Amar Nath Raina, and Dr. Ali Mohammad went immediately to see him. He complained of light pain on the side of left chest, lower part. Temperature was 99.2 degrees, pulse 90, pleuritic friction of heat of left infraxillary region; diagnosis dry pleurisy. Dr. Mookerjee gave history of an attack of dry pleurisy in 1937, of relapse in 1944. A proper treatment including antibiotics was administered. His condition improved and he felt much better afterwards. Still, as a precautionary measure, he was kept under medical supervision.

On the morning of 22nd June, Superintendent of Jail, received a telephone call from Guru Dutt Vaidya, who was staying with Dr. Mookerjee, informing him that Dr. Mookerjee had an attack of pain in the chest followed by perspiration. Accordingly, Dr. Ali Mohammad, with the Superintendent, Central Jail, hurried to the villa, reaching there at 7 a.m.

On enquiry, the history given was of pain in the heart area, lasting for about two minutes. He had perspiration and sensation of fainting. He was fully conscious. Immediate restorative measures were given and his condition improved. It was decided to shift him to the nursing home in the state hospital, Srinagar. Dr. Ali Mohammad was with him up to 9 a.m. and when he saw that the patient's condition was better, he hurried to the hospital in order to make necessary arrangements for his reception in the nursing home. The medical officer, jail dispensary, was left there to watch the patient.

At noon, Dr. Mookerjee was taken to a comfortable car

from the villa to the nursing home. The medical officer, jail dispensary, was left there to watch the patient.

At noon, Dr. Mookerjee was taken to a comfortable car from the villa to the nursing home. From the main gate of the hospital he was carried in a wheelchair up to the lift and then again in the same wheelchair he was carried up to his bed in the nursing home.

As has already been stated in the medical report issued by the government on 23rd June, 1953, he was examined in the nursing home by two physician specialists, namely, Dr. Ali Mohammad, M.R.C.P. (*Edin.*) and Dr. Ramnath Parhar, M.D. (*Edin.*). All examinations and investigations including electro-cardiogram were made and a provisional diagnosis of heart attack of coronary type was made. The patient related that he had a similar attack in the year 1937 and once again a few years later. Appropriate treatment was prescribed including sedatives, antibiotics and aminophylline. Patient's condition was fairly good. He was kept under constant nursing and medical attendance.

When asked whether he would like his relatives to be informed about his removal to the nursing home, Dr. Mookerjee said that he would prefer to inform them himself. At about 2 p.m. on 22nd June he sent the following telegrams:

1. To Justice Mookerjee, 77, Asutosh Mookerjee Road, Calcutta.

   "Sudden dry pleurisy three days ago. Better today. Fever and pain much less. Removed to hospital. Satisfactory medical arrangements made. No anxiety. Specially tell mother—Syama Prasad."

2. To Anutosh Mookerjee, Somamoy Boring Road, Patna.

   "Sudden dry pleurisy three days ago. Much better today. Removed to hospital. Satisfactory medical arrangements. No anxiety—Bapi."

3. To Mrs. Banerjee, 30, Altamont Road, Bombay.

"Sudden dry pleurisy three days ago. Pain and fever less today. Removed to hospital. No anxiety. Inform Hasu *Bowma* and see they do not worry—Syama Prasad."

At 7.30 p.m. Dr. Mookerjee was seen by the District Magistrate, Srinagar, and Mr. Trivedi, his counsel. The surgeon specialist, Dr. Girdhari Lai Kaul, who is also the Assistant Superintendent of the hospital was present. Dr. Mookerjee appeared quite cheerful at the time and while attending to some work, such as dictating notes to his counsel and signing cheques, he cut jokes with those present.

At 9 p.m. his general condition was fairly good, except for low blood pressure, i.e. 102-80 as recorded by Dr. Ali Mohammad.

At 11 p.m. the patient felt restless and oxygen was administered. At this time, his blood pressure was 100-80 as taken by Dr. Jagannath Zutshi, the house surgeon, who was in attendance. Glucose with aminophylline was given intravenously.

His condition improved subsequently as recorded by Dr. J.N. Zutshi, house surgeon. However, at I a.m. Dr. Mookerjee had a setback and his condition did not improve thereafter. The end came suddenly at 3.40 a.m. and Col. Moitra and Major Mehta of the Indian Army Hospital and Dr. Chopra, whose help had been requisitioned, arrived at the nursing home a few minutes too late.

It has already been stated that Sardar Hukam Singh met Dr. Mookerjee on 16th June and found him 'quite all right'. Further, Col. Sir Ram Nath Chopra has mentioned in his report that Dr. Mookerjee "remained in perfect health up to June 19." It is thus evident that till June 19th, Dr. Mookerjee was in a satisfactory state of health.

I have shared the facts with the public. The tragedy developed with a swiftness no less unexpected in Kashmir than in other parts of the country. In this common sorrow, there is no room for recriminations, for, despite all efforts, a great figure has passed away.

D

MAULANA AZAD'S STATEMENT ON 23.6.53

Maulana Abul Kalam Azad in a statement said he had learnt with deep sorrow of the death of Dr. Mookerjee.

"Whatever be our political differences with Dr. Mookerjee," he said, "the hand of death has wiped them out. What we remember today vividly are his fine qualities and the record of his service to the country."

Maulana Azad said: "I have learnt with deep sorrow that Dr. Syama Prasad Mookerjee died early this morning in a nursing home at Srinagar. He caught a chill three days ago which developed into dry pleurisy. The government of Jammu & Kashmir immediately transferred him to a nursing home and arranged that his friends present in Srinagar should be by his side. His condition deteriorated and at

1 a.m. he had a heart attack. At 3.30 a.m. he passed away. The Government of India have arranged a special plane to carry his body to Calcutta.

"I understand the government of Jammu & Kashmir are issuing a communique with necessary details.

"We remember today vividly his fine qualities and the record of his service to the country. My personal relations with Dr. Mookerjee date back to 1935. We have been friends since then and our friendship has endured in spite of all political differences.

"I would like to convey my condolences to the members of his family in their bereavement."

—*Amrita Bazar Patrika,* 24th June 1953

E

SH. ABDULLAH'S SPEECH ON 26.6.53

Shrinagar, June 26: Kashmir Premier, Sheikh Abdullah, said here yesterday that the death of Dr. Syama Prasad Mookerjee was an unfortunate occurrence. Sheikh Abdullah said Dr. Mookerjee's death was all the more regrettable because the government was considering to send him to Delhi immediately after Shri Jawaharlal Nehru's return to India.

The Kashmir Premier was addressing the Delhi teachers' goodwill mission now touring the Valley.

Referring to the circumstances under which the Jan Sangh leader was detained and arrested in the state for defying the permit system, Sheikh Abdullah said even though "the permit system means some difficulty for us, we have to submit to tihe needs of the national security of India as defence of the country is paramount for every Indian."

The Premier added that though technically Dr. Mookerjee was under detention "The government had allowed him all facilities, particularly in view of his weak state of health."

He said, Dr. Mookerjee had "moved to the nursing home reluctantly as he felt that his ailment was not serious."

—U.P.I.

—*Hindustan Standard,* 27th June, 1953

F

MR. JAWAHARLAL NEHRU'S STATEMENT (EXTRACTS)

"I was on the point of leaving Geneva by air for Cairo when I heard the news of Dr. Syama Prasad Mookerjee's deathi. The news stunned me as it was wholly unexpected. About a month earlier, I had paid a brief visit to Srinagar. I had made enquiries then about Dr. Mookerjee, about his health and where he was kept. I was told that he was keeping very well and I was shown where he was staying. This was a lovely villa by the side of the Dal Lake and adjoining the famous Moghul Garden called the Nishat Bagh. The villa had a little garden with fruit trees and flowers. From the accounts I had, I was happy to learn that Dr. Syama Prasad Mookerjee was living in healthy and agreeable surroundings and was being well looked after. I had hoped that, in these conditions and in the excellent summer climate of Srinagar, he would improve in health.

"The shock, therefore, of the news of his death was all the greater because it was so utterly unexpected. He and I had often differed in our views in regard to political matters and we have had many an argument in Parliament. But however much we differed, we respected and had affection for each other and his passing away is a severe loss. Parliament, of course, will be much poorer. We are poor enough in men of outstanding ability at a time when the country demands all that is best in us.

"The fact that Dr. Syama Prasad Mookerjee died in detention makes his end particularly sad and painful. The Kashmir government went all out to treat him with every courtesy and to offer him every convenience that was possible in the circumstances. To them, his death was a severe blow. The end came suddenly. It is easy for all of us to be wise after the event and to point out what should have been done and was not done. But till the very evening preceding his death, no one suspected what was going to happen and Dr. Mookerjee himself met his lawyer friend that day and sent reassuring telegrams to his relatives in Calcutta, telling them not to worry.

"Within a few days of his death, Dr. Mookerjee had long interviews with Sardar Hukam Singh, his lawyer, and Pandit Prem Nath Dogra of the Praja Parishad. He was discussing with them, so I am told, the question of withdrawal of the movement with which he had become associated.

"The Kashmir government had decided to release him within a few days, but that was not to be, and tragedy supervened and found another release for him.

"I can well understand the shock that his numerous friends and others experienced when they heard of this sad event for which they were so totally unprepared. But sorrow should not lead us astray from right and balanced thinking. It should lead us rather to a deeper and calmer consideration of even wider issues. A leading personality amongst us has passed away and the burden is all the greater on those who remain..."

—*Hindustan Standard,* 3rd July, 1953

G-1

STATEMENT OF SHRI GURU DUTT VAIDYA A CO-DETENU WITH DR. MOOKERJEE; DATED 25.6.53

We, Dr. S.P. Mookerjee, Shri Tek Chand, myself and others, started from Delhi on the 8th May morning. Dr. Mookerjee issued a statement containing the purpose of Dr. Mookerjee's going to Jammu. It was to find out facts there, to see some persons there and to find out ways and means by which further action for the settlement of Kashmir issue may be taken. During our tour in the Punjab, Dr. Mookerjee sent a telegram from Ambala to Sheikh Abdullah. In that telegram he expressed his intention to go to Jammu to find out ways and means for settling Jammu & Kashmir problem. He also pressed his desire to see Sheikh Abdullah, if possible. Dr. Mookerjee sent a copy of the telegram to Shri Nehru as well. After the two days' tour of the Punjab, on the 10th evening, when we were boarding the train from Jullunder, a gentleman sitting inside the compartment got himself introduced Dr. Mookerjee as District Magistrate of Gurudaspur. He informed Dr. Mookerjee that he would not be allowed to reach Pathankot. He had instructions of the Punjab government to be ready to arrest him. Of course, he could not say the time and place where he would be arresting him as he was waiting for further instructions. The Gurudaspur District Magistrate was coming from Simla after attending a conference.

At Phagwara on 9th May, Dr. Mookerjee had already received a reply to his telegram from Sheikh Abdullah (copy of which is attached). When we entered Gurudaspur district on the 11th and at Batala, the local S.D.O. entered our compartment, remained sitting with us and introduced himself to Dr. Mookerjee. But he told him that he had not come to arrest him but simply to escort him through his area. His area was over at Gurudaspur and the S.D.O. of Gurudaspur came and sat by us when the first man left. He went with us up to Pathankot. At Pathankot, the District Magistrate and many other officials were present on the platform but they did not arrest us nor did they speak to us. At about 12 o'clock, a message came from the District Magistrate, Gurudaspur, to the place where we had been staying to the effect that he wanted to see Dr. Mookerjee. So he came at about 1 p.m. He informed Dr. Mookerjee that he had received a message from his government to allow him and his party to proceed to Jammu, in spite of the fact that Dr. Mookerjee and his party had no permit. He offered help to procure conveyance, etc. for us to go to Jammu. In fact one of his subordinate officers took some of the persons of the party in his jeep up to Madhopur check-post. At Madhopur check-post the District Magistrate and all his officers were standing and the District Magistrate wished us good journey. The driver of our jeep had at that time complained that he had no permit to enter Jammu state. We demanded a permit from the District Magistrate. He stated that we should proceed and the permit would follow us. So we proceeded but when we had traversed half the Ravi Bridge, Jammu police officers and a good many constables were found to be standing there and one Mr. Aziz, Superintendent of Police, Kathua, informed Dr. Mookerjee that he had to perform a very unpleasant duty to ask him not to proceed further as his government had issued an order prohibiting his entry in Jammu & Kashmir state and he showed the order. Dr. Mookerjee told him that he had been allowed by the Indian Government to go into the Jammu & Kashmir state and he would proceed to that place.

On this the Superintendent of Police produced another order from his pocket, arresting him. On my and Shri Tek Chand Sharma's declarations that we were also going to Jammu with Dr. Mookerjee, Mr. Aziz told us that we were also under arrest without showing us any order. At Lakshanpur post we were kept for about half an hour and one gentleman saying that he was the Inspector-General of Police, Jammu & Kashmir state, told us that we both were under arrest and he read an order from the paper. And after that myself, Shri Tek Chand Sharma and Dr. S.P. Mookerjee were made to sit in a jeep and under police and military escort consisting of a captain and, some Kumaon regiment soldiers, were taken to Jammu and from there to Kashmir.

We reached Udampur at 10.30 p.m. where we took our

night meals in a dakbungalow. Dr. Mookerjee expressed that he was feeling very tired and he also said that he was in the habit of sleeping early. So he would like to stay there instead of proceeding further. But the officer-in-charge, that captain, told us that there was no room in the dakbungalow available and they had got a room reserved for us by telephone at Batote dakbungalow and we had to go there. So after half an hour's stay there, we proceeded to Batote and reached there at about 2 a.m. So we stayed at Batote for the rest of the night. We started from Batote after taking the morning tea at 7.30. We reached Kazikundu at about 1 p.m. There we took our lunch and started from there at about 2 p.m. and reached the Central Jail, Srinagar, at 3 p.m. After preliminary enquiries, etc. we were taken to a cottage near Nishat at about 4 p.m. There the Superintendent of Jail, the District Magistrate, Srinagar and Dr. Ali Mohammad came to see us. They all enquired about Dr. Mookerjee's health and then we were allowed to stay there.

Three days after our arrival there, Dr. Mookerjee fell ill of pain in the right leg and he had temperature. We had no thermometer and therefore we could not say what his temperature was. The doctor came the next day and prescribed Belladonna plaster and a mixture for taking in. What the prescription of the mixture was, we did not know. It was sent from the hospital. He expressed his opinion that it would be better if Dr. Mookerjee was taken to the hospital and he would speak to the authorities. For three or four consecutive days another doctor, named Premnath, came and applied plaster. Dr. Mookerjee was all right in four or five days' time. After a fortnight Dr. Mookerjee fell ill again of the same trouble, having pain in the leg and fever. Dr. Ali Mohammad came again and prescribed Belladonna. Another doctor came and applied this Belladonna. Dr. Mookerjee was all right after two or three days.

Dr. Mookerjee had been constantly complaining to the Superintendent of the Jail, to the Inspector-General of Prisons and to District Magistrate, Srinagar, that there was no sufficient space to walk inside the bungalow and he might be given permission to go out for at least an hour a day. In fact, the Superintendent of Jail and the Inspector-General of Prisons allowed him to do so under police escort. But the police did not obey them and Dr. Mookerjee was never given an opportunity of going outside. The police in-charge wanted a written order from the Superintendent of Jail and it was never sent. We heard from Mr. Trivedi when he came for interview on 16th June that permission for taking him out for a walk had been given but the actual order never reached there till Dr. Mookerjee fell ill for the third time.

On the night between the 19th and 20th June, Dr. Mookerjee felt a pain in the back and he had high temperature. In the morning when we saw the temperature on the thermometer, it was 99.4° and the pain was acute. The doctor was called. He came at about 11.30 and examined Dr. Mookerjee. He declared that Dr. Mookerjee was suffering from dry pleurisy and prescribed a streptomycin injection and some powders, the prescription of which was not shown to us. The doctor said that his blood and urine ought to be tested but this was not done so long as Dr. Mookerjee was up to the point when he was removed to the hospital. The doctor advised that he might take two powders a day and if the pain is acute, he might take more of them up to six.

Dr. Mookerjee told the medical officer, Mr. Ali Mohammad that his family physician, Dr. Bose had advised him not to take streptomycin because it does not suit his system. On this, Ali Mohammad said that this advice was given long ago and now we know much better about this drug. So Dr. Mookerjee need not worry, he would be all right. The medicine came at about 3.30 p.m. and the injection, full one gram was given. One powder was also given. The doctor left five remaining powders saying that he would take at least one and if need be, more at night. The injection was given by the jail doctor and not by Ali Mohammad.

Dr. Mookerjee told the Superintendent that news of his illness should be sent to his relatives. That night Dr. Mookerjee was feeling very restless but by the morning, the pain was a little less and the fever also a little lower than what it was the previous morning. On that day at about 10 o'clock in the morning the jail doctor came and gave another injection of streptomycin, one gram, and supplied more powders. After the injection had been given in the morning by the jail doctor, no other medical man either the jail doctor or Dr. Ali Mohammad, had come to see Dr. Mookerjee on that day or in the night until the next morning, i.e., 22nd June as stated later on. The Sub-Inspector of Police in charge came in the afternoon to Dr. Mookerjee to enquire how he was and got the information as above.

There was no arrangement made by the doctor for nurses in the sub-jail. In the evening at about 4 p.m. the pain increased and fever also increased a little up to 100.2°. In the night at about 11.30 on 21st June, Dr. Mookerjee felt that the pain was increasing and according to the instructions of the doctor, he took another powder. I left his room after 11.30 when he felt sleepy.

Next morning, i.e. 22nd June, I was awakened by the jail servant, at about quarter to 5, who told me that Dr. Mookerjee wanted me immediately. I went into his room and found him to be fainting, perspiring and looking very depressed. I checked his pulse. It was very feeble and his whole body was very cold. Dr. Mookerjee told me that he was perspiring for the last half an hour and feeling giddy as if he was going to faint. Dr. Mookerjee also told me that he slept from about midnight to about 4 in the morning when he woke up with the pain in the heart region and with perspiration. At first he thought that he would recover without disturbing anybody but finding the trouble increasing and was about to faint, he called the servant. He had called him several times as he could not get up.

The sub-jail was a small bungalow with three small rooms at a distance of about 7 miles from Srinagar and about 10 miles from the hospital where Dr. Ali Mohammad is stated to be living. We immediately gave to Dr. Mookerjee a little *dalchini* and a little sugar, *labanga* for sucking and in five minutes' time Dr. Mookerjee began to feel better and in about 15 to 20 minutes' time the perspiration had stopped, the pulse had become stronger and the heart pain was also decreasing.

At that time I asked the *hawaldar* to telephone the Superintendent of Jail to send for the doctor and the *hawaldar* took me with him and I telephoned to the Superintendent at the Central Jail between 5.15 and 5.30 and gave him the particulars of Dr. Mookerjee's condition. He informed me that he was coming with the doctor immediately. There was no telephone at the place where we were staying. There was only one telephone at the waterworks office which is closed, except during the office hours. So it took some time to get somebody to open it. The Superintendent came with Dr. Ali Mohammad at about 7.30 p.m. He examined Dr. Mookerjee. At that time Dr. Mookerjee was feeling better. The body had become warm except the fingertips. Dr. Ali Mohammad stated that pleurisy was much better and it was on account of low blood pressure and of lowering of the temperature that this heart trouble had been felt. The temperature of Dr. Mookerjee was 96.8° in the mouth but at about 5.15, the perspiration had stopped and the body was getting warm. When the doctor examined him, the temperature was 98° under the tongue.

Dr. Ali Mohammad gave him a coramine injection, 2 c.c. on the arm. Dr. Ali Mohammad had another doctor with him at that time. Dr. Mohammad asked the other doctor to get a syringe ready with 2 c.c. coramine but the doctor said 2 c.c. would be too much for one injection. To that Dr. Mohammad said that Dr. Mookerjee had a very heavy body and 2 c.c. is all right, and then he told Dr. Mookerjee that he was asking the authorities to remove him to the hospital.

I asked the Superintendent of the Jail to allow us to stay with Dr. Mookerjee in the hospital. At least one of us should be allowed to remain with Dr. Mookerjee in the hospital. He said that that was not possible. Dr. Ali Mohammad said: "I understand your anxiety but you need not worry, he will be perfectly safe in our hands." I asked the Superintendent of Jail to take one of the jail servants who had been serving Dr. Mookerjee in the jail for the last few weeks to the hospital to serve him there also. The Superintendent said that it was not necessary. The Superintendent of Jail also told us that it would not be possible for him to arrange for our food in the hospital as arrangement would be made for Dr. Mookerjee's diet.

Dr. Ali Mohammad left us, asking the Superintendent to take Dr. Mookerjee in an ambulance to the hospital. The jail doctor remained with us. At about 10, Mr. Trivcdi came and saw Dr. Mookerjee. After consulting Dr. Mookerjee about the case he left at about 11 and the Superintendent with the motor car came to us at about 11.30. Dr. Mookerjee was removed in a chair from his room to the car standing outside the bungalow and then he was taken away in a small four-seater car, which was very uncomfortable for a heart patient.

We did not hear anything about Dr. Mookerjee till 7.30 in the evening. At 7.30 a telephone call came for me and I had to go to the place where the telephone was installed and the Superintendent of Jail told me that he was coming from the hospital and Dr. Mookerjee was feeling much better.

Next day, the 23rd June, the Superintendent of Jail woke me at about quarter to 4 in the morning and wanted me, Mr. Sharma and Prem Nath Dogra who was also staying with us for the last three days to accompany him to the hospital immediately. I asked him what was the matter. He told me that he had been asked by the D.M. on telephone to take us to the hospital without telling him what for. He himself did not know anything else.

We started at about 5 minutes to 4 a.m. and reached the hospital at about 4.30 and there I was informed by Mr. Trivedi who was already there, that Dr. Mookerjee had expired. After 10 minutes, I asked for permission of the doctor to go into the room and see the body myself. I, Shri Tek Chand Sharma and Prem Nath Dogra went into the room and saw the body. By that time the body was all cold. When we were coming out of the room Shri Tek Chand Sharma asked a nurse who had followed us into the room "at what time Dr. Mookerjee expired?" The nurse replied at 2.30 a.m. She also added that Dr. Mookerjee at about 1 a.m. expressed his wish to have his companions with him.

Two days previous to the last illness, Dr. Mookerjee had lost appetite and was taking very little food. From the day it was declared that he was suffering from pleurisy and that doctor said that he could take anything he liked, but Dr. Mookerjee took only tea, coffee and vegetable soup. On the 20th and 21st he took two cups of vegetable soup and one or two cups of tea and a cup of coffee in a day. He took a little orange juice also on the morning of 22nd on the advice of the doctor.

It is a matter of regret that a precious life was lost in circumstances which I feel could admit of more efficient handling.

(a) Medical assistance was not available on the spot where Dr. Mookerjee was detained even when his condition became serious.

(b) No nursing arrangements were at all made in the place of detention.

(c) No laboratory tests were made so long as he was in the sub-jail.

(d) None of his fellow detenus were permitted to be at his bedside when he was removed to the hospital. Even after Dr. Mookerjee expressed the desire that his fellow prisoners should be brought to the hospital, no information was sent to them till he passed away.

(e) No intimation was at all sent by the Kashmir authorities to Justice Mookerjee, his mother and his other relatives, nor was any attempt made to have the service of an independent competent medical practitioner.

(f) In spite of Dr. Mookerjee's protest based on competent medical advice during his previous illness at Calcutta, streptomycin was administered to him without a previous pathological examination or without consulting his Calcutta doctors, who were available on the phone.

G-2

STATEMENT OF SHRI U. M. TRIVEDI, COUNSEL FOR DR. MOOKERJEE; DATED 25.6.53

I met Dr. Mookerjee for the first time on the 12th inside the cottage where he was kept in detention. I was accompanied by the District Magistrate and after a few formal words of greetings, I asked Dr. Mookerjee to move to a room where I could get instructions from him in private, after he had so moved into the room. The District

Magistrate who had accompanied me informed me that the government had instructed him to allow instructions to be given entirely in his presence and within his hearing. I immediately refused to have any such instructions and took the District Magistrate with me where Dr. Mookerjee was sitting and conveyed to him the conditions under which the interview was being granted. He agreed with me and he also refused to give instructions. I therefore left Dr. Mookerjee, but at that interview I formed an impression that he was not looking cheerful. On my return to hotel, I was interviewed by some press reporters and conveyed my idea of his not being cheerful which I think was reported by the *Hindustan Standard.*

I again met Dr. Mookerjee on the 18th at 9 o'clock. I had free discussions with him for about three hours and I drafted a petition for him and also an affidavit to be sworn in the presence of the District Magistrate. He did not like the idea of my suggesting that Dr. Mookerjee was not cheerful because he felt that probably his family might construe it in some different light. At this interview he was quite jolly and I conveyed to him the information which was given to me by the government that his request for taking him out for a walk had been granted.

I again saw Dr. Mookerjee on the 22nd morning at about 10 o'clock before I reached the place of detention I was informed by the Superintendent of Jail that Dr. Mookerjee was not feeling well and under instructions of the doctor he was to be removed to a nursing home and arrangements were being made to remove him there. I enquired from him where this nursing home was. He was very reticent and did not disclose the whereabouts of the nursing home. My interview with Dr. Mookerjee on this day lasted for about an hour, from 10 to 11.

I found him reclining in bed, but he looked quite cheerful. He mentioned to me that probably he would have passed away in the early hours of the morning—"*Mere bhai panch baje to chale jata tha.*" It was then only that the seriousness of his illness was felt by me. I enquired from him how he was feeling then. He told me that he had no pain and was feeling quite all right. However, I did not feel very satisfied. I told him, as it was time for me to attend the court, I would then leave him, but see him positively in the evening again. I left Dr. Mookerjee at about 11 and on my way to the court, I met the Superintendent and another gentleman coming in a small car. The Superintendent informed me that he was going to bring Dr. Mookerjee and take him to a nursing home. I then went to the court and there I found I had left some reference books in the hotel. So I sent Mr. Devki Prasad—that young friend of Dr. Mookerjee who had made an application there—to fetch the books from my hotel. This was about mid-day. Devki Prasad, on returning, told me that he saw Dr. Mookerjee being carried in a small car towards the city and he also informed me that there was no nursing home in the direction in which the car was going.

After the Court work was over at about 5.15 p.m. I contacted the District Magistrate and asked him to take me to the place where Dr. Mookerjee had been kept. Before that I had sent out at least five young men to hunt out practically all known nursing homes if any was anywhere near and

I received information that in none of the nursing homes Dr. Mookerjee was kept. In the meanwhile, the District Magistrate came down to me in his own car and picked me up to take me to Dr. Mookerjee. I was taken to the state hospital, about three and a half miles from my hotel and I was taken to Dr. Mookerjee in room No. 1 of gynaecological ward of that hospital on the first floor. I found Dr. Mookerjee in bed in a reclining condition. He looked very pale, though smiling. I remarked to him that he was not as well as he was in the morning. But he would not accept that. He said that he was feeling a little better. Then the District Magistrate gave him all his letters (about 15 or so in number). He went through all the *dak*, one of which was a telegram from Poona, from one Meera. I read out that telegram to Dr. Mookerjee.

I then enquired of him if he wanted me to send out some telegrams to his relatives or to Hashi at Poona. He informed me that he had already despatched three telegrams through the District Magistrate. The District Magistrate was standing by my side. He confirmed sending the telegrams And I further enquired from Dr. Mookerjee if he wanted anything more to be said in those telegrams. He said nothing more was required to be said and there was no cause for any particular anxiety. At that time there were certain papers from some firm in liquidation and Dr. Mookerjee sat up in the bed, took up his fountain pen and went through that correspondence and signed about six or seven statements and two cheques.

Then he asked me to write down a letter to one Sailen. He joked with me, saying, "Your handwriting is bad; I can read it, but none else can, so how can I dictate letters to you?" etc. I wrote out the letter and he signed that letter. At that time the doctor who was present there inside the room and the Medical Superintendent, Girdharilal asked me to convey to Dr. Mookerjee that he should not try to sit up in bed. After signing that letter, he again reclined and at the time of reclining, he placed his hand on his heart and his face indicated that he felt some pain.

I had some idle talk with him and continued to sit with him right up to 7.15 or 20 p.m.; may be above 25 also. I did not feel very happy about his condition. I took the doctor a little away and enquired how did he feel about the condition of Dr. Mookerjee. He said there was nothing to be afraid of; the crisis, if any, had already passed and the next morning he would be X-rayed and he further told me that within two or three days he would be quite fit.

However, I did not feel satisfied even then, because I did not like the look of Dr. Mookerjee. I was thinking of going away the following morning by plane to Pathankot, but I cancelled my idea and told him that unless I saw him quite happy on the following morning, I would not leave. When I was parting company at about 7.30 or so, he asked me to bring some periodicals for him. I asked him what particular type of literature he wanted. Then be said anything that interested me would interest him also. He was also a human being, and anything that interested others would surely interest him also. He could also read what I could.

"Bring anything, but do bring something and spend some money over it." I then placed my hand on his in order to feel if there was any temperature. I found it normal and I left him with a promise to return the next morning.

Inside the room I found one nurse who was always standing by and outside the room I found some police guards posted. So I requested the District Magistrate to allow me to visit him at about 9 in the morning. But the doctor suggested that I should come at about 8 as he would be X-rayed at about 9 o'clock. The District Magistrate asked the guard on duty to allow me to come. At this interview of mine, the petitioner on behalf of Dr. Mookerjee had accompanied me and he was also allowed to see Dr. Mookerjee.

Next when I heard about Dr. Mookerjee was only at about quarter to four in the early morning of 23rd. The Superintendent of Police informed me that Dr. Mookerjee's condition was rather serious and the District Magistrate had asked me to come to the hospital to be by the bedside.

I immediately went there, reaching there at 5 minutes to four. I found the door of Dr. Mookerjee's room closed and one doctor seated in the visitors' room. I was asked to sit by his side, but I became restless as I could not tolerate sitting like that. So I enquired within a minute about the condition of Dr. Mookerjee.

The Superintendent of Police, of course, said that oxygen was being given. Then I told him, "Let us go and sit inside the room; go and find out whether I could go in." He went inside the room and returned with the doctor who informed me that Dr. Mookerjee had passed away five minutes before my arrival in the hospital.

Then I was taken into the room. I found the body covered up. I removed the cloth from above his head and found him dead.

Within 5 minutes of my arrival, the District Magistrate

arrived there and the Deputy Home Minister also arrived. I had a talk with the Deputy Home Minister. I informed him then and there that I would like to take the body to Calcutta and he must make arrangements. And if he cannot, he must allow me to contact the Government of India.

He promised me he would be able to do that. I then asked him to send messages to his family members immediately and contact his Calcutta house so that the news may be broken to his mother, not by any announcement from All-India Radio, but by some of his relatives concerned. I also asked him to send for the co-detenus and he informed me that they had all been sent for. While I was still at the hospital, all three of them arrived. I gave them the news and as the Home Minister Mr. Bakshi Ghulam Mohammed had already arrived there, I asked him to release all the detenus who were there and allow them to accompany me in the aeroplane. He, therefore, asked them to be carried back immediately and get their things packed.

This was at about 4.35 a.m. The Deputy Home Minister had already gone to convey the news. I also returned to my hotel at about 4.50 a.m. and I phoned up All-India Radio man and the *Times of India* representative as well as the U.P.I. man, and asked them to come to my hotel. The *Times of India* man and the All-India Radio man arrived within 5 minutes and I conveyed this news to them. Till then they did not know anything.

I then tried to make a telephonic call to Delhi to Mouli Chandra; I could not get him. Then I tried to get a call to Jammu, but I did not get it. I was informed by the All-India Radio man that he had tried for full two hours and he also did not get any connection. At about 8 o'clock, again I went to the hospital and met the Deputy Home Minister. Then he told me that he could not get a direct phone call to Calcutta, but he was able to talk with Justice Mookerjee through the operator and he also sent messages to Bombay through Delhi. He also told me that he had already talked to Dr. Katju before 5 a.m.

In the meantime about 500 people came to the hospital and gathered at the front gate; and so the body was taken through the back door.

About 8 o'clock, I asked for his things. I got his wristwatch, fountain pen and a suitcase; the attache case was not there. There was no key, nor any lock to the suitcase. *Chappals* were lying outside. The specs were there, but not the case.

After we left for the aerodrome at about 8.40, the police staff who happened to be all Hindus—the Superintendent, the Deputy Superintendent, Sub-Inspector and one head constable—did not like the idea of Mohammadan staff touching the body.

The police officers suggested that if the body had to be lifted to the stretcher, I might make a suggestion that their services should be utilised for the purpose, and Mohammadans need not touch. So I asked the District Magistrate to call the detenu friends. I had also asked for their release and also requested the Home Minister to release Prem Nath Dogra also who was undergoing a long sentence of imprisonment.

I asked the District Magistrate to arrange for the release of these gentlemen before the body could be lifted, because

I felt that at least 10 men would be required to lift the body. At 8.40, these three detenus arrived, but before their arrival, the body was brought out with the help of the police officers and the military officers. We carried the body to the ambulance, and all of us who lifted the body sat inside the ambulance itself. We reached the aerodrome by 9.5.

At the aerodrome, all the ministers except the Chief Minister, Sheikh Abdullah, were present. At that time practically all the ministers expressed their very great regret; the Finance Minister broke down, the District Magistrate also again broke down. The Chief Minister arrived at about 10.15 a.m. In between there appeared to be some obstruction by the Indian Government, authorities about the use of the Indian Air Force Dakota. The Wing Commander and other officers on the spot were willing to help, and were awaiting orders from the air headquarters to fly. Mr. B.B. Ghosh of Defence Ministry was phoned up; he was not contacted. For about half an hour obstructive messages were being received from the headquarters, Delhi.

The Home Minister then asked the Deputy Home Minister to contact Dr. Katju.

When Dr. Katju was contacted, the Home Minister himself talked for about 10 minutes and asked Dr. Katju to talk to the Wing Commander then and there and get subsequent ratification from the Defence Ministry for the use of the Indian Air Force Dakota. The weather was extremely bad; the Civil Aviation had stopped its planes from proceeding and Dr. Katju did not feel willing to lend the Dakota.

Then Bakshi Ghulam Mohammed told him that (I was

standing by the side and listening to the talk) he must not refuse. Then Dr. Katju spoke to the Wing Commander, but I could not make out what was communicated to him for even after his phone, the Wing Commander refused to lend the plane. Bakshi Ghulam Mohammed got wild with him and made him to obey his orders, taking the full consequence on himself.

While this telephonic communication was going on, Sheikh Abdullah arrived. All the ministers then joined in lifting the stretcher and put it in the plane after placing wreaths. Sheikh Abdullah brought a special flowered shawl and placed it on the body. We left the aerodrome at 10.40 a.m. under the impression that we will get down at Delhi, wherefrom another plane will take us to Calcutta.

After we passed Kashmir state territory, I was informed by the pilot that he had instructions to proceed to Jullunder. Then I told him why not to Ambala? He told me that the landing ground at Ambala was not good. But at Jullunder he received no instruction to land. He tried to get instructions on the radio, but he could not. We reached Jullunder at 12.30. The plane hovered around Jullunder for half an hour, left Jullunder without landing, proceeded 50 miles to the south, returning back to Jullunder again; again left Jullunder and landed at Adampur Airport at 2 p.m.

At 2 o'clock when we get down, I met the pilot of I.N.A. plane there. I enquired how he happened to be there. He was to take off at Delhi. He said that he was sorry. Home Minister had instructed him to pick up here and so he had come. "I have to refill—that I do not know where—and then proceed to Calcutta."

We left Adampur at 2.30 p.m. and got flown to the military airport at Kanpur.

We got down there and after refill we left again at 5.30 p.m. At Kanpur we calculated the distance to Calcutta, and we found out that still we had 500 miles to fly. The officer told me that we would not reach Calcutta before 9 p.m. He would, however, try his best, but he would not be able to reach before 9 o'clock. We reached Calcutta at 5 minutes to 9 p.m.

After reading the statement of Pandit Guru Dutt Vaidya and comparing it with my personal knowledge, which I have put down in my statement, the following salient features, are noticeable:

1. Mookerjee was not advised complete rest after the first attack on 22nd morning, 4 o'clock.
2. He was not immediately removed to the hospital while seven valuable hours were lost.
3. He was not carried to the hospital in an ambulance but was carried in a small taxi and in uncomfortable position.
4. The immediate medical relief was not made available even after entry into the hospital.
5. The gravity of the illness was not noticed.
6. The Superintendent, Jail, was asked to remove Dr. Mookerjee to the hospital early morning but he wasted time and actually sat chatting with Mr. Raina for nearly one and a quarter of an hour.
7. The medicine that was given to relieve his pain was not well-studied with relation to Dr. Mookerjee's heart trouble.

8. When the doctors knew that he had heart trouble, they failed in doing their duty to issue a bulletin immediately and to study the case with the greatest care possible, specially when it appeared to be a case of heart trouble.
9. All causes of mental pain ought to have been removed—the posting of police guards at his room and not allowing him the congenial company of one of those who knew him was also bad.
10. The treatment for pleurisy might be called expeditious but was symptomatic and not in a studied relation to the physical condition of Dr. Mookerjee and his past medical history;
11. The diagnosing doctor left it in the hands of his junior to carry out his behest without reference to Dr. Mookerjee and notwithstanding his suggestions to give him smaller doses of streptomycin and avoid the use of sedatives.

H

MEDICAL EXPERTS' OPINIONS ON KASHMIR GOVERNMENT COMMUNIQUE

Dr. N.B. Khare, M.D.

Dr. Khare, in a statement on 25th June, 1953, said, "After carefully studying the communique issued by the Kashmir government along with the medical report on the illness of late lamented S.P. Mookerjee, I am constrained to say that the treatment given appears to me to be faulty for the following reasons:

1. The patient, who was apparently suspected to be suffering from heart-attack—coronary type—should not have been removed from his residence; removal in such cases is always contra-indicated.
2. At 12 noon on the 22nd instant at the nursing home when a diagnosis of coronary attack was made, aminophylline, which is the recognised treatment for coronary attack, should have been given immediately. Why was its administration delayed till 11 p.m., i.e. for eleven hours?
3. Blood pressure was found to be low, that is 100/80 and after aminophylline was given, it was found to have gone lower, that is 90/70. Why was not anti-shock treatment given and measures taken to raise blood pressure, e.g. intravenous injection of dextran by drip-method?"

—*Hindustan Standard,* 26th June, 1953

Dr. N.B. Khare, in a statement on 3rd July, further said, "The lengthy and revised communique of the Kashmir government on the death of Dr. S.P. Mookerjee not only gives no answer to my previous charge, but serves to justify and strengthen the nationwide demand for a deep probe into the affairs."

"Medically, this lengthy statement," Dr. Khare said, "is an ingenious attempt to evade the charges levelled by me in my last statement of the 25th June. But the staggering anomalies in the statement have served to defeat the very purpose for which it was issued. Besides the inadequacy of the treatment pointed out by me, I have some more lapses to point out."

Dr. Khare said, "Dr. Mookerjee was supposed to be under care of the physician specialist, Dr. Ali Mohammad. It was he who handled the case from the very start. But it is strange that Dr. Ali's name does not appear anywhere after 9 p.m. on the 22nd June when he last recorded the blood pressure, which was found to be low. After 9 p.m. the case was in charge of Dr. J.N. Zutshi, a house surgeon and a person, who was never known to have attended on Dr. Mookerjee. The very fact that the help of the military doctors and Dr. Chopra was requisitioned, though late, lends support to the contention that medical attendance was inadequate and that the attending doctor was at his wit's end. That the doctors arrived after the death means they were informed very late and not at 1 p.m. when the setback occurred. It may be that the doctors were out of the station or else the seriousness of the situation was not impressed upon them."

Dr. Khare pointed out: "From the main gate of the hospital he was carried in a wheelchair up to the lift and then again in the same wheelchair up, to his bed in nursing home... Since a wheelchair was found to be necessary to handle the patient, why was one not used to carry the late doctor from his room in the villa to the car?" he asked. "This means that he was made to walk from his room to the car and this is sheer neglect or callousness. Such patients are not carried in a sitting posture but in a lying position on a stretcher," Dr. Khare added.

"According to the .statement Dr. Syama Prasad was taken to the nursing home at 12 noon and at 2 p.m. he wrote a telegram to Justice Mookerjee. It is also mentioned that the tests were carried out and a provisional diagnosis of heart attack (coronary type) was made. The telegram makes no mention of this. Also, the authorities enquired whether they should inform his relatives about the transfer and, mind you, not about the heart attack, the diagnosis of which was made previously.

"News of the transfer of Dr. Mookerjee was flashed in the press on the 23rd morning. The bulletin said that he was afflicted with dry pleurisy. Since the transfer and diagnosis took place between 12 noon and 2 p.m. on 22nd, the Kashmir government knew at the time it handed over the news about the transfer to the press agencies that the late doctor was suffering from a serious and dangerous ailment, viz. heart attack of the coronary type, a disease in which the end is always sudden. Why was this then not mentioned in the news flash? Besides no reason is given as to why was Justice Mookerjee not informed about the affliction even of dry pleurisy, which certainly is not a minor ailment, on the 20th or 21st or even of the heart attack on the 22nd," Dr. Khare said and added that the nationwide demand for a deep probe into the affair was fully justified.—(FIT)

—*Hindustan Standard*, dated 5th July, 1953

Dr. Nalini Ranjan Sen Gupta, M.D.

Analysing the medical report on Dr. Mookerjee's death as embodied in the Kashmir government's press communique Dr. Nalini Ranjan Sen Gupta made the following points:

1. During the first 10 days of his illness, reported by Mr. Justice Rama Prasad Mookerjee and published in newspapers, no medical treatment had been arranged—at least no information of such

treatment had been available. For better medical facilities, Dr. Mookerjee should have been sent to India or medical aid should have been rushed to him from India.

2. During the first 10 days of illness Dr. Mookerjee should have been removed to a better climate.
3. Dry pleurisy had been diagnosed on the morning of 20th June. He passed a very restless and sleepless night on 20-21 June. In spite of this, it appears that no constant medical aid had been arranged during the day and the night following which he was seized with that severe attack with symptoms of collapse at 4 a.m. on 22nd morning. It appears from the communique that in spite of information to the jail authorities, no doctor had arrived till 7.30 a.m.
4. Dr. Mookerjee's condition was clearly one of coronary thrombosis. All the time between the 20th morning and 6 a.m. of 23rd, even after his death, the official knowledge in Kashmir was that Dr. Mookerjee had died of pleurisy and not of coronary thrombosis. Therefore, the story of the doctor having diagnosed the case as coronary thrombosis is either a concoction or was not seriously considered. This is borne out by the fact that the patient was carried 10 miles away to the city—a procedure unthinkable in a coronary case where restorative measures had to be taken at 7.30 a.m. The narration of the facts suggests that

the doctor never diagnosed it as coronary and it was only an afterthought.

5. To keep a man so obviously ill with such a fatal illness in charge of people who cannot even diagnose such severe attacks and if diagnosed, handle him so roughly like a quack, is a blunder which definitely cost the patient's life and cannot be condoned or pardoned.
6. The attending physicians, in practically giving a copy-book line of treatment adopted in coronary thrombosis, never mentioned morphine or anti-coagulants. No doctor worth the name can think of treating coronary thrombosis without anti-coagulants. And as to morphine, it is the sheet-anchor in our treatment. Pethidine is only a poor substitute and even that was given at 1 a.m., 18 hours after the attack. It seems therefore, that the doctor either did not diagnose it as coronary thrombosis or if he did, he was so ignorant of modern methods of treatment that he was the last man to be put in charge of a coronary case.
7. If coronary thrombosis had been diagnosed, many accessory treatments might have been done which were not done at all.

Dr. Amal Kumar Roy Chowdhury, MJD.

Giving his opinion, Dr. Amal Kumar Roy Chowdhury said it seemed to him that the diagnosis of the disease by the attending physicians was incorrect. He made the following observation on the Kashmir government's press communique:

Dry pleurisy is really secondary to the extension of inflammation from the heart to the pleura and as such, the original heart-trouble, it seems, started several days back. In fact, extension of inflammation from one region to the other takes some time. Dry pleurisy may also be secondary to an attack of pneumonia and both these conditions—pneumonia and coronary—particularly at this age in a patient having a previous history of coronary attack—are very very serious.

Before removal to hospital, 10 miles away from his place of detention, nothing appears to have been done to record the pulse rate, blood pressure, respiratory rate in the sitting and in the recumbent posture. These should have been noted before removal to the hospital.

As regards treatment, accepting that it was a case of coronary attack, detected by electro-cardiograph, the best method of treatment would have been to prevent the shock generally associated with this type of trouble, not by pethidine injection but by stronger drugs, namely, morphine, provided there was no contra-indication to the use of such drugs. Then also the prothrombin have been noted and injection and anti-coagulant drugs should have been given, not aminophiline. Pethidine was administered at 1 a.m. If pethidine was administered at all, it should have been given earlier, just when complaints of pain over the heart were made and not several hours after, as stated in the press communique.

Then there was no detailed report on blood and urine examination. At a stage of shock with a fall in blood pressure and rapid pulse, intravenous injection was generally contra-indicated.

So it seemed there must have been bungling somewhere and that proper attention had not been paid to the case.

—*Hindustan Standard,* dated 28th June, 1953

Dr. T. N. Bannerjee

Patna, June 23: On hearing the sad news of the death of Dr. S.P. Mookerjee, MP and Jan Sangh leader, Dr. T.N. Bannerjee, M.L.C. said: "I was stunned on hearing the news. We read in the paper this morning that Shri Syama Prasad Mookerjee has developed pleurisy but no one dreamt that an intellectual giant and a true patriot of our country will die so soon from a disease which, when timely diagnosed and properly treated with modern up-to-date medicines, saves 99 per cent of its victims.'

—*Searchlight,* dated 24th June, 1953

Ajmer Doctors' Comment

Ajmer, June 29: A board of eminent doctors headed by Dr. Ambalal Sharma have issued the following joint press statement regarding the treatment given to Dr. Mookerjee prior to his death:

"Without entering into political aspects of Dr. Mookerjee's death, we simply comment as medical men on the line of treatment which was adopted by Dr. Ali Mohammad as reported in the press.

"In our opinion a patient of coronary attack should not have been removed from his bed at any cost, and the latest treatment for heart attack should have been undertaken at the earliest diagnosis.

"Aminophyline is indicated only in the initial stages of the attack, whereas it was given intravenously when the blood pressure was 100 and the patient was in a state of collapse. As a rule, Aminophyline lowers the blood pressure and its intravenous use may prove dangerous in such a condition. We have been using the latest and established drugs, such as khellin, lacharnol, cardiazol and cordarone, etc. in our practice. Treatment for collapse, such as plasma, glucose intravenous, etc. was not given. Opinions may differ but in our long practice of 40 years, we have come across a number of cases successfully treated. If a patient dies suddenly, it is a different matter but if time permits, which it certainly did in the case of Dr. Mookerjee, we have known that this type of treatment is lifesaving.

"Without casting aspersions on anybody, we have given our opinion as above and invite the opinion of other professional experts on the subject."

—*Hindustan Standard,* dated 30th June, 1953

I

STATEMENTS OF SOME EMINENT PERSONS ASKING FOR ENQUIRY

Dr. M.R. Jayakar

Poona, June 23: Observing that Dr. S.P. Mookerjee's death would shock the country, Dr. M.R. Jayakar said: "To die in prison-house locked there by his country's *swadeshi* government, by persons with whom he shared power as a colleague only a few days ago, is a fitting termination of a warring life. Let us hope that this incident will make the Government of India realise, in their self-complacent enjoyment of the chits of American visitors, the deep enormity of their behaviour which ignored all the canons of fairness and justice accepted by a civilised government."

Shri Purushottam Das Tandon

Allahabad, July 1: Shri Purushottam Das Tandon, former Congress president, today supported the demand for an enquiry into the death of Dr. S.P. Mookerjee in Srinagar.

Shri Tandon, who was presiding over a meeting here convened by the Akhil Bharat Banga Sahitya Sammelan, said he felt that Dr. Mookerjee's treatment was not properly done. Shri Tandon hoped the Government of India would explain the whole situation after due enquiry.

The Kashmir government, Shri Tandon said, should have given Dr. Mookerjee all the facilities to visit Kashmir and study the situation there.

Speaking "with full responsibility", Shri Tandon said the people of India were not able to know what was happening inside Kashmir. There was an 'iron curtain' over the land and even newspapers could not write what they knew.

—P.T.I.

Hindustan Standard, dated July 2, 1953

Shri Jayaprkash Narayan

Shri Jayaprakash Narayan, Praja Socialist leader, said here (at Lucknow) yesterday that the Kashmir authorities were 'criminally negligent' in looking after Dr. Syama Prasad Mookerjee's health.

The Praja Socialisl leader, in a statement issued, said: "I regret deeply that the Prime Minister, in his reply to Shri Atulya Ghosh, as reported in the press this morning, has stated so categorically that there was no negligence shown by the Kashmir government in the care of the late Dr. Syama Prasad Mookerjee.

"I cannot say what facts have been placed before the Prime Minister, but the facts as I know them, lead to an entirely different conclusion.

"I was at Calcutta only three days ago, when I took the opportunity of calling on Dr. Mookerjee's family to offer my condolences and my homage to the departed leader.

"It was on this occasion that Mr. Justice Rama Prasad Mookerjee told me the whole story, as he, a distinguished jurist, had been able to piece together. The story left no doubt in my mind that the Kashmir authorities were not only negligent but criminally negligent in looking after Syama Babu's health. I feel sure that the life of this great Indian could have been saved by better care."

Shri Jayaprakash Narayan added, "It seems to me that after such a national tragedy the least that the Indian government could do was to institute a proper and impartial enquiry into the whole affair. Meanwhile, it does not seem proper for the Prime Minister to pronounce judgement on such a controversial subject and to attempt to whitewash the guilt of those who seem to deserve severe punishment."

Shri Narayan added that he had no intention to say anything about this matter. But he was afraid that the expression of the Prime Minister's opinion might lead to a grave injustice and he thought it was necessary to challenge it publicly.

—*Hindustan Standard,* dated 9.7.53

Dr. B.C. Roy

West Bengal Chief Minister Dr. B.C. Roy has drawn the attention of Prime Minister Shri Jawaharlal Nehru to the rising public feeling in West Bengal over the question of death in detention of Dr. Syama Prasad Mookerjee in Kashmir, it is learnt.

Referring to the public demand for an enquiry into the circumstances of Dr. Mookerjee's death, Dr. Roy, in a communication to the Prime Minister, is understood to have stated that the situation called for an enquiry by eminent non-official persons like Dr. M.R. Jayakar or Shri Hriday Nath Kunzru or a Supreme Court judge and that such a step alone could allay mounting public feelings. Dr. Roy had left it to Shri Nehru as to how best to tackle the situation.

Dr. Roy is further understood to have drawn the attention of the Prime Minister to what was described by the public as the callousness of the Kashmir government towards medical treatment of Dr. Mookerjee.

Hindustan Standard, dated 1.7.53

In a telegram to Dr. Roy on the occasion of his birthday, Sheikh Abdullah stated:

"Please accept my heartiest congratulations on your auspicious birthday. I wish you many happy returns of the day. I understand you are leaving for Europe shortly. I would like to remind you of your promise to visit Kashmir this season.

"I would be delighted if you could come up before your departure for Europe. Incidentally, your visit at this juncture would help the opportunity of acquainting yourself with the details on the spot."

The following is the text of Dr. Roy's reply:

"Your telegram reached me today, July 3, contents of which had already appeared in the press even before its receipt by me. Thanks for your good wishes on my birthday and also your kind invitation to visit your place.

"I am grateful also for offering me the opportunity to acquaint myself with details regarding Dr. Syama Prasad Mookerjee's sad demise. To get acquainted with such details I must, besides visiting Srinagar, also meet those friends who were associated with Dr. Mookerjee during his last illness and at the time of his death. Many of these friends may not be in Kashmir now. I am leaving for Europe on the day after tomorrow as my doctor will not be available after July 10. I may immediately, on return, contact these friends and associates and also go over to Kashmir.

While I may undertake this task, I would prefer some non-political persons to do the job. If you do not approve of this suggestion of mine, you may allow one or two such persons to be associated with me when I take up the job myself. Such information as we can thus jointly collect will, I feel, satisfy the public more effectively. Meanwhile, may I suggest you to preserve all documents, case sheets and other materials regarding Dr. Mookerjee's illness and death."

Shri H.V. Kamath

(Extracts from a speech delivered at Nagpur)

Why was he not released when he fell ill a fortnight ago and his condition did not improve; when were his relations informed, what medical facilities were provided? Many such questions naturally arise. He said, "What looks *prima facie* like awful bungling demands an immediate independent inquiry. As he was a distinguished Opposition leader of Parliament, I suggest the inquiry should be conducted by an all-party committee of Parliament nominated by the Speaker and not weighted by a Congress majority. The committee can be constituted straightway though Parliament is not in session."

Mr. Kamath added, "If Sheikh Abdullah has nothing to hide, he should welcome the inquiry. If he resists, Parliament should consider the adoption of stern measures against him and his government. I trust Prime Minister Nehru will rise above petty personal and party considerations and act quickly. Let us meanwhile strive for the cause of national unity for which Dr. Mookerjee so valiantiy laid down his life," concluded Mr. Kamath.

—UPI

—*Hindustan Standard,* 26th June

Pandit Prem Nath Dogra

Urging the appointment of an impartial commission to enquire into the circumstances of Dr. Syama Prasad Mookerjee's death in detention in Kashmir, Shri Prem Nath Dogra told a press conference in Calcutta on Tuesday that the facts as he knew them and the information that had reached him from different sources had convinced him that this was a case of deliberate negligence. There was a mystery about it which could be resolved only by the appointment of such a commission of enquiry.

Referring to Prime Minister Shri Nehru's statement expressing satisfaction at the arrangements made to save Dr. Mookerjee's, life, Shri Dogra said, "It was his duty as the Prime Minister to ascertain facts before he pronounced his opinion. He and others who were with Dr. Mookerjee in the Srinagar sub-jail could give him facts, but he had not cared to enquire about these from any of them. It is now, therefore, the duty of the people to press him for the appointment of an impartial commission of enquiry. That is the one thing that will give some consolation to the afflicted mother of our departed leader," he said.

—*Hindustan Standard,* 15th July

Shri S.S. More

(From a speech at a public meeting held at Poona on 23.6.53)

Shri S.S. More (Peasants and Workers Party), paid tributes to Dr. Mookerjee for the unparalleled work he did in the Parliament. "Like a colossus he stood there in the defence of democracy," he said. Shri More wondered why Dr. Mookerjee was not released from detention the very moment his health was disturbed. He hoped that Prime Minister Nehru would make proper inquiries and explain the entire position to the country. Mr. More said, he personally felt that the Kashmir government was ill-advised in detaining him.

—*Hindustan Standard,* dated 25th June, 1953

Pandit Hridaynath Kunzru

A largely attended public meeting at Sholapur, which was presided over by Pandit Hridaynath Kunzru, asked the Government of India to "officially inquire into the circumstances leading to the death of Dr. Mookerjee in Srinagar."

—Extracts from *Amrita Bazar Patrika,* dated 25th June, 1953

Srimati Sucheta Kripalani

Extract from a speech delivered by Smt. Sucheta Kripalani, MP at a public meeting held in Calcutta on 23rd July, 1953:

Demanding an enquiry into the circumstances leading to Dr. Mookerjee's death, the Praja Socialist leader, Srimati Sucheta Kripalani, MP, expressed surprise how a leader like Dr. Mookerjee could die in detention and under such circumstances as had been reported in free India today.

***

"Along with their demand for an enquiry into the death of Dr. Mookerjee the public should also demand repeal of the Preventive Detention Act, she said. If the government did not institute an enquiry into the matter, they would believe that there was some mystery in Dr. Mookerjee's death, which the government wanted to hide," she added.

—*Hindustan Standard,* dated 24th, July 1953

Shri N.C. Chatterjee

Mussoorie, July 9: In a statement here tonight, Mr. Chatterjee said, "Unless it has a guilty conscience, no government should resist the demand for an impartial enquiry into events leading to the death of any detenu in detention."

Mr. Chatterjee said, "The mystery into Dr. Mookerjee's death is daily deepening as facts are emerging. There are serious misgivings in the public mind on losing the precious life of a great Indian due to carelessness of a government, whose policy he had criticised and resisted.

"Millions share Mr. Jayaprakash Narayan's deep regard at the non-response of the Prime Minister to the demand for an enquiry and his pronouncing an ex parte judgement in favour of the Kashmir government. This judgement, the country is not going to accept."

Mr. Chatterjee added, "The demand for an inquiry is not from so-called communalists but also from eminent persons like Shri Purushottam Das Tandon, Acharya Kripalani, Dr. B.C. Roy and Dr. Jayakar. Prime Minister Nehru should realise that there is a deep-rooted suspicion in the public mind that his government was as much responsible as the government of Sheikh Abdullah for Dr. Mookerjee's incarceration in Srinagar.

"With a full sense of responsibility, I say that there is a *prima facie* case of gross negligence. Sheikh Abdullah feels it, otherwise he would not have asked Dr. Roy to proceed to Srinagar and inquire into facts.

"The government should appoint a commission to hold an independent inquiry immediately as Dr. Roy will be out for a considerable period."

—PTI

—*Amrita Bazar Patrika,* dated 11th July, 1953

J

CORRESPONDENCE BETWEEN SHRI ATULYA GHOSH AND MR. JAWAHARLAL NEHRU

The 29th June, 1953
No. WC/4 237/8

Dear Panditji,

I am placing before you the feeling of some of the members of the Provincial Congress Committee as well as my own feelings.

According to reports received uptil now, we find that the serious nature of the illness of late Dr. Syama Prasad Mookerjee were made known to the authorities of Kashmir government on the early morning of 22nd. But it is amazing that no intimation was sent to his family members nor to his physician Dr. B.C. Roy by the authorities concerned. The Kashmir government appears to be callous.

The way the news was communicated to the house of Dr. Mookerjee was highly objectionable. A telephone message was given to Justice Rama Prasad Mookerjee conveying the news that Dr. S.P. Mookerjee was dead. No other information was sent and it was said in a blunt manner. It seems that there was no consideration for the feeling of the aged mother. You know late Dr. Mookerjee was an eminent person and he was highly respected in our province, if not in the whole of India. From reports published in the newspaper, it seems that no facilities were given to him for his treatment nor his sons or daughters were informed about his continued ill health, nor any request was made to the members of his family to visit him while ailing under detention. The public feeling in our state has risen very high. I do not want to suggest anything to you but I think some kind of enquiry by eminent non-official persons, such as Dr. Jayakar or Shri Kunzru or a Supreme Court judge will be helpful to us. Of course you know best how to tackle the situation.

I am sending a copy of this letter to Dr. B.C. Roy.

Your sincerely,
Atulya Ghosh

Pandit Jawaharlal Nehru,
Prime Minister,
Government of India, New Delhi

New Delhi
July 2, 1953

My dear Atulya Babu,

I have your letter of the 29th June.

I am aware of the feelings in Bengal in regard to the death of Dr. Syama Prasad Mookerjee. I think that this is largely due to lack of knowledge of the facts. I have gone into these matters carefully and I am quite convinced insofar as the Kashmir government is concerned, they did everything in their power to show courtesy and consideration to Dr. Syama Prasad Mookerjee. The Health Minister of the Kashmir government, Shri Sham Lal Saraf, has issued a statement giving some facts which have appeared in today's papers. You will, no doubt, see this. It is, I think, completely unjustified to say that the Kashmir government's attitude was callous. It was the very reverse of this.

Right from the beginning of Dr. Mookerjee's detention

in Kashmir he was treated with extraordinary courtesy and a lovely villa was placed at his disposal. There is no better place in the whole of India for a person to choose to live in. There was the lake in front and nearby was a famous Moghul garden. Everyone who was with Dr. Mookerjee or who went to see him spoke highly of the way the Kashmir government provided for his comfort.

When he felt somewhat unwell on the 22nd, even then no one suspected that his case was serious. He was taken to the hospital so that he may have better treatment. The doctors there wanted to send information to his family, but Dr. Mookerjee himself asked them not to do so and he sent telegrams himself to three members of his family in Calcutta. There is no doubt that these telegrams were sent. I have seen the photostat copies of the originals. You will see that neither the Kashmir government nor the doctors were to blame in this matter. Later, the same evening his lawyer, Trivedi, saw him and had a talk with him and showed him a number of papers. Till then also, no one suspected any dangerous developments. It was only about 11 o'clock at night that his condition began deteriorating. The doctors were in attendance throughout. There was some improvement, but again there was deterioration. Information was sent to a minister of the Kashmir government, who hurried out of his bed and went to the Indian Army Station Hospital to bring doctors from there. Distances are great in Srinagar and these doctors arrived just when Syama Babu was dying or had died.

I do not see what else could have been done. It may be said that information might have been sent a little earlier in the night. No one in the Kashmir government was aware of the serious development till long after midnight.

You refer to the way news was communicated to Justice Mookerjee by telephone. As a matter of fact, it took a long time to get the telephone connection. After this was obtained, it was impossible to talk directly as nothing could be heard. The minister who was on the line in Srinagar, Durga Prasad Dhar, ultimately had to ask the Delhi operator to give the message to the Calcutta operator, who repeated it to Justice Mookerjee. You can well imagine what happened to the message in the course of this double relay. It must have been distorted and only the briefest message was given. I have had a talk with Durga Prasad Dhar, who says that he gave a long message, but naturally only a distorted form went through. I am sure that Justice Mookerjee, if he is informed of this, will realise that absolutely no discourtesy was intended. Indeed, the ministers of the Kashmir government were very greatly upset by Syama Babu's death. They had been thinking of releasing him soon.

Yours sincerely,
Sd/- Jawaharlal Nehru

Shri Atulya Ghosh,
President,
West Bengal Pradesh
Congress Committee,
59-B, Chowringhee Road,
Calcutta 20

K

CORRESPONDENCE BETWEEN LADY MOOKERJEE AND MR. JAWAHARLAL NEHRU

No. 499—p.m.—New Delhi June 30, 1953

My dear Mrs. Mookerjee,

It was with deep grief that I learnt a few days ago, as I was leaving Geneva for Cairo, that your son, Dr. Syama Prasad Mookerjee, had died. The news came as a shock to me for, though we may have differed in politics, I respected him and had affection for him. To you, his mother, the shock must have been very great and I can say little to lessen your sorrow.

I sent a telegram from Cairo to Dr. Bidhan Chandra Roy, asking him to convey my deepest sympathy and condolences to you. It is a matter of particular sorrow to me that Syama Babu's death should have occurred as it did under detention. When I went to Kashmir about five weeks ago, I enquired particularly as to where he was kept and about his health. I was told that he was being kept, not in any prison, but in a private villa on the side of the famous Dal Lake in Srinagar. I found that the Kashmir government was anxious to give him such comfort and amenities as were possible and that he was keeping well. I was happy to learn this at the time. Indeed, I hoped that the healthy climate of Kashmir might lead to an improvement in Syama Babu's health.

But it was not to be so and the shock and sorrow are, therefore, all the greater. I suppose it was beyond human power to do anything and we have to bow to circumstances beyond control.

To you, revered lady, I offer my respectful homage and expression of sorrow. If I can be of any service to you, you will please not hesitate to inform me.

Yours sincerely,
Sd. Jawaharlal Nehru

77 Asutosh Mookerjee Road, Calcutta
4th July, 1953

Dear Mr. Nehru,

Your letter dated 30th June was forwarded to me on the 2nd of July by Dr. Bidhan Chandra Roy.

I thank you for your message of condolence and sympathy.

The nation mourns the passing away of my beloved son. He has died a martyr's death. To me, his mother, the sorrow is too deep and sacred to be expressed. I am not writing to you to seek any consolation. But what I do demand of you is justice. My son died in detention—a detention without trial. In your letter you have tried to impress that the Kashmir government had done all that should have been done. You base your impressions on the assurances and information you have received. What is the value, I ask, of such information when it comes from persons who themselves should stand a trial? You say, you had visited Kashmir during my son's detention. You speak of the affection you had for him. But what prevented you, I wonder, from meeting him there personally and satisfying yourself about his health and arrangements?

His death is shrouded in mystery. Is it not most astounding and shocking that ever since his detention there, the first information that I, his mother, received from the government of Kashmir was that my son was no more and that also at least two hours after the end? And in what a cruel, cryptic way the message was conveyed! Even the telegram from my son that he had been removed to the hospital reached us here after the tragic news of his death. There is definite information that my son had not been keeping well practically from the beginning of his detention. He had been positively ill a number of times and for successive periods. Why did not, I ask, the government of Kashmir or your government send any information whatsoever to me and my family?

Even when he was removed to the hospital, they did not think it necessary to immediately intimate us or Dr. Bidhan Chandra Roy. It is also evident that the Kashmir government had never cared to acquaint itself with the previous history of Syama Prasad's health and provide for nursing arrangements and emergent medical attendance in case of need. Even his repeated attacks of illness were not taken as a warning. The result was disastrous. I have positive evidence to prove that he had, to quote his own words, a 'sinking feeling' on the morning of 22nd June. And what did the government do? The inordinate delay in getting any medical assistance, his removal to the hospital in a most injudicious manner, the refusal to allow even his two co-detenus to be by his side in the hospital, are some glaring instances of the heartless conduct of the authorities concerned.

The responsibility of the government and their own doctors cannot be in any way evaded or lightened by some stray quotations from Syama Prasad's letters chosen at random, that he was keeping well. What is the value of such quotations? Does anybody seriously expect that he—of all persons—and that while in detention far away from his dear and near ones—would ventilate his grievances through letters or diagnose his own malady? The responsibility of the government was immense and serious.

I charge them that they had utterly neglected and failed to discharge this bounden duty. You speak of the comforts and amenities given to dear Syama Prasad in detention. It is a matter to be enquired into. The Kashmir government had not even the courtesy to allow free flow of family correspondence. Letters were held up with inordinate delay and some mysteriously. His anxiety for home news, particularly of his ailing daughter and my poor self, was distressing. Will you be astonished to learn that on the 27th June last, we received here his letters dated 15th June, despatched by the Kashmir government in a packet on the 24th June, that is, a day after sending his dead body? That packet also brought back to us the letter addressed by myself and others here to Syama Prasad which had reached Srinagar on the 11th and 16th June, but had never been delivered to him. It was purely a case of mental torture. He had been repeatedly asking for sufficient space for walking. He was feeling ill for want of it. But he was persistently refused it. Is not this a method of physical torture too? I am filled with surprise and shame to be told by you "that he was being kept, not in any prison but in a private villa on the side of the famous Dal Lake in Srinagar." Strictly confined in a small bungalow with a little compound, guarded day and night by a body of armed guards—such was the life that he was leading. Is it seriously maintained that a golden cage should make a prisoner happy? I shudder to hear such desperate propaganda. I do not know what medical treatment and assistance had been given to him. The official reports, I am told, are self-contradictory. Eminent physicians have expressed their views that it was, in the least, a case of gross negligence. The matter requires a thorough and impartial enquiry.

I do not bewail here the death of my beloved son. A fearless son of free India has met his death while in detention without trial under most tragic and mysterious circumstances. I, the mother of the great departed, demand that an absolutely impartial and open enquiry by independent and competent persons be held without delay. I know nothing can bring back to us the life that is no more. But what I do want is that the people of India must judge for themselves the real causes of this great tragedy enacted in a free country and the part that was played by your government.

If a wrong has been done anywhere, by any person, however high he may be—let justice take its course and let the people be cautious so that no mother in free India has again to shed tears with the same agony and grief that has befallen me.

You are good enough to tell me not to hesitate to inform

you about any service that you may render to me. Here is the demand on my own behalf and on behalf of the mothers of India. May God give you courage to allow truth to see the light.

Before I close my letter, I would refer to one very important fact. Syama Prasad's personal diary and his other manuscripts/writings were not returned by the Kashmir government along with his other belongings. Copies of correspondence between Bakshi Ghulam Mohammed and my eldest son, Rama Prasad, are enclosed herein. I shall be deeply grateful if you could recover the diary and the manuscripts from the Kashmir government. They must be with them.

With my blessings,

Yours in grief,
Sd/- Jogmaya Debi.

New Delhi,
5th July, 1953

Dear Mrs. Mookerjee,

I thank you for your letter of the 4th July which has just reached me. I can well understand a mother's sorrow and mental anguish at the death of a beloved son. No words of mine can soften the blow that you must have felt.

I did not venture to write to you before without going into the matter of Dr. Syama Prasad's detention and death fairly carefully. I have since enquired further into it from a number of persons who had occasion to know some facts. I can only say to you that I arrived at the clear and honest conclusion that there is no mystery in this and that Dr. Mookerjee was given every consideration.

I might mention that letters to Kashmir go by air, but the air services are very irregular because of the weather and sometimes they do not go for a week or more. In fact, they have not gone there now for over a week and many important letters which I had sent have thus been delayed.

It has been my lot to spend about ten years in prison and I have been kept in innumerable jails of all kinds all over India, and so I know something about how a prisoner feels and what the conditions of his imprisonment usually are.

On the day of Dr. Mookerjee's sudden death, a minister of the Kashmir government tried to telephone to Justice Mookerjee. It was not possible for him to get through for a long time, and then he could not speak directly. His message was relayed by two operators on the way and no doubt became completely distorted.

I am forwarding your request about Dr. Mookerjee's diary and other papers to Bakshi Ghulam Mohammed. I am sure that, if he has got any papers, he would certainly send them.

Yours sincerely,
Sd/- Jawaharlal Nehru

Dear Mr. Nehru

Your letter dated 5th July reached me on 7th.

It is a sad commentary on the whole situation. Instead of helping to clear up the mystery, your attitude deepens it. I demanded an open enquiry. I did not ask for your 'clear and honest conclusion'. Your reaction to the whole affair is now well known. The people of India and I, the mother, have got to be convinced. There is a rooted suspicion in the mind of many. What is required is an open, impartial, immediate enquiry.

The various points raised in my letter remain unanswered. I had clearly told you that I had positive evidence to prove certain very relevant and important facts. You do not care to know or look into them. You say that you had enquired "from a number of persons who had occasion to know some facts." It is strange that even we—the members of his family—are not regarded as persons who can throw at least some light on the matter! And yet you call your conclusion to be 'honest'!

Your reference to the irregularity in the Kashmir air-mail service is of no avail. That does not explain the total disappearance of letters and the inordinate delay in many cases. If you had taken pains to go through my letter with care, you would have, I am sure, hesitated to offer such a lame excuse. Post-marks on the covers of the letters we hold positively belie your theory in the present case.

Your experience in jails is known to all. It was at one time a matter of great national pride with us. But, you had suffered imprisonment under an alien rule and my son has met his death in detention without trial under a national government. What would have happened if such a tragic and mysterious end had come behind the prison bar during the British rule?

It is futile to address you further. You are afraid to face facts. I hold the Kashmir government responsible for the death of my son. I accuse your government of complicity in the matter. You may let loose your mighty resources to carry on a desperate propaganda, but truth is sure to find its way out and one day you will have to answer for this to the people of India and to God in heaven.

I am releasing our correspondence to the press. Let the people of India judge and act when their Prime Minister fails.

Yours in grief,
Sd/- Jogmaya Debi

CORRESPONDENCE BETWEEN BAKSHI GHULAM MOHAMMED AND SHRI RAMA PRASAD MOOKERJEE

Copy of telegram sent to Bakshi Ghulam Mohammed on 28th June, by Shri Rama Prasad Mookerjee.

Bakshi Ghulam Mohammed
Home Minister
Srinagar (Kashmir)

Do please send immediately Syama Prasad Mookerjee's personal diary and manuscript/writings not sent with the body and any ether personal belongings that are still there.

Rama Prasad Mookerjee

Copy of letter confirming the above telegram written on the same day.

77, Asutosh Mookerjee Road,
Calcutta-25
The 28th June, 1953

Dear Mr. Ghulam Mohammed,

I have sent the following telegram to you today:

"Do please send immediately Syama Prasad Mookerjee's personal diary and manuscript/writings not sent with the body and any other personal belongings that are still there."

Syama Prasad had been regularly keeping a diary and it was with him while in detention at Srinagar. It is a black bound book. He had also been writing some literary work there. The diary and the manuscript/writings have not been sent with his other belongings that came with his body. There may be other personal articles still lying at Srinagar.

I earnestly request you to send immediately all those articles, particularly the diary and the manuscripts without fail. It is needless to explain the value we attach to these articles.

Your personal attention to this matter will be much appreciated.

Yours sincerely,
Sd/- Rama Prasad Mookerjee

Copy of the telegram from Mr. Bakshi Ghulam Mohammed, Home Minister, Kashmir, dated 29th June.

X R SRINAGAR KMR 29 RAJ 37
Justice Rama Prasad Mookerjee, Calcutta

IS/2374/D/53 Your telegram stop all personal belongings of Syama Prasad Mookerjee carried by Tek Chand, his personal secretary and Mr. Trivedi his counsel please contact them—Bakshi, Home Minister.

Copy of letter from Shri Rama Prasad Mookerjee to Bakshi Ghulam Mohammed dated 3rd July, 1953.

77, Asutosh Mookerjee Road,
Calcutta 25,
The 3rd July, 1953

My dear Mr. Ghulam Mohammed,

I am greatly surprised at the reply you have sent. As I said before, the personal belongings that were sent by you with Syama Prasad's body did not include his diary and manuscript/writings. Syama Prasad, we know, had been regularly keeping his diary while in detention at Srinagar. It must have been with him at the hospital. It is most surprising and regrettable that it was not sent along with his other belongings. Messrs Tek Chand and Trivedi informed us that they had brought only those articles that had been handed over by the Kashmir authorities. Some articles had been handed over to Mr. Trivedi at the hospital but they did not contain the diary. We also know that Syama Prasad had been writing a good deal in detention. Curiously enough, the articles sent by you do not include any of his manuscripts as well.

I earnestly entreat you again to find out his diary and the manuscripts immediately and send them to us.

Yours sincerely,
Sd/- Rama Prasad Mookerjee

L

AN ARTICLE REPRINTED FROM THE *ORGANISER*, DATED 20TH JULY, 1953

The Prime Minister has been pleased to state that he has enquired "from a number of persons who had occasion to know some facts" and come to the conclusion that martyred Dr. Mookerjee had been lodged in a nice bungalow and that he "was given every consideration".

We have also enquired from a number of persons who had occasion to know many facts. Some of these facts we have published. Here are some more.

The house in which the beloved leader was lodged is not a 'fine bungalow'. It is neither fine nor a bungalow. It is a ramshackle cottage. It is not a government building. It is a private house. But it is so desolate and derelict that no tourist has ever cared to hire it. *It is unfit for human habitation.* Nor is it true to say that it is located on the banks of the Dal Lake. It is not even on the main road. *The surroundings are as wild as they are weird.* They look like belonging to some other planet than ours. The house itself is full of owls and snakes. Abdullah put a few ricketty cots into this reeking house and also put our dear Syama Prasad in it.

More than once Dr. Mookerjee saw snakes creeping by him. Often he complained of them to the gardeners. The helpless gardeners could only answer with looks of mute embarrassment. The house is exposed to gusts of snowy winds from the surrounding mountains. It was nothing short of criminal to keep a man from the plains with previous heart trouble, in a bleak snake-pit like this. According to a report of the gardeners, Doctorji often complained of the cold. He asked for warm clothing from the jail authorities. It was some days before Bakshi sent in an overcoat and some blankets.

The cold desolation of the place soon affected his health. He complained of pain and sickness to the jail authorities. *But the only medical attention he got was from a sub-assistant surgeon (L.M.P.) in charge of the sub-jails of Srinagar. So that in the beginning he was treated no better than hundreds of other prisoners.*

When Dr. Ali Mohammad examined him on the morning of June 22, he is reported to have passed adverse remarks on his medical treatment.

At about 12 noon a small transport van No. 159 carried Dr. Mookerji to the nursing home. *He was made to walk up to the van and later made to sit up in it without even pillow support or blanket cover.* The Jail Superintendent sat to his right as though to remind him that he was Abdullah's prisoner. He was seen in this position by several persons near Nedou's Hotel.

Before leaving the prison-house, Dr. Mookerjee thanked the menial staff and expressed his gratitude by folding his hands. Of course, it is well-known that none of his co-detenus was permitted to accompany him.

In the evening when Shri Trivedi and Shri Devki Prasad called on him in company with the D.C., no doctor, and only one nurse, was in attendance on him. During the half hour they were with him, he received no treatment of any sort.

His room in the so-called nursing home was a cubicle

12×12, ill-equipped and ill-furnished. In this small room he was confined, with Abdullah's armed policemen standing guard. One cot, one old half-brocken chair and one stool constituted the entire furnishings. The D.C. seated himself on a stool and made Shri Trivedi sit on the chair; Devki Prasad kept standing. At the instance of Dr. Mookerji, a chair was found for him.

Dr. Mookerji besmeared his hand with the black paint of the cot on which he was lying. He tried to wash it off with water. Water failing to wash it, he asked for soap. *However, in this hospital not a soap cake could be found.* Ultimately he asked the nurse to take one out of his attache case, which she did.

It is learnt that the doctor in charge of the ward in which Dr. Mookerjee was put, was on leave. So that Dr. Zutshi of another ward was asked to do a side job with Dr. Mookerjee. Dr. A.H. Mohammad and Dr. Parhar who are mentioned in the Abdullah communique as having waited on him, were, in fact, not residing on the premises. Their residences are far removed from the hospital. Latest enquiries have revealed that none of these specialists waited on him on that fatal night.

To the nurses who called on him at 9.30 p.m., he complained about the unworthy treatment meted out to him by Abdullah. He said that when he became well and went to India, he would expose the tyranny of Abdullah.

Only one nurse, Rajdulari Tiku, was in attendance on him. When he felt like passing urine, he called her as his daughter and was sorry that she should hold the urinal for him. According to Rajdulari, the dying leader cried in agony for a doctor but none was at hand. She rushed Noor Ahmed, a scavenger, to call in Dr. Zutshi. Dr. Zutshi came running in, but found the patient in a grave condition. He rang up Dr. Ali for instructions. Meanwhile his condition deteriorated and he passed away at 2.25 a.m. *Dr. Ali arrived more than half an hour after death. The whole communique time of death as 3.40 a.m. is absolutely false.* They spent the one hour and a quarter fabricating forms to fit in with the communique. *The whole communique is a tissue of lies.* When the nurse found that the worst had already happened, she burst into loud lamentation.

Later, ministers were called in. Conspicuous by their absence was Abdullah and his pro-Pakistani minister, Afzal Beg.

Is the Prime Minister still satisfied that nothing was left undone to save the priceless life of our Syama Prasad?

□

Appendix-II

The following two notes, written in Dr. Mookerjee's own handwriting were found in his briefcase, which he had left locked up at the sub-jail, when he was removed to the hospital. The first one is a temperature chart, kept by him, for 20th, 21st and morning of 22nd June. The second one is, presumably, a note prepared by him in connection with his application before the Kashmir High Court.

1

Temperature Chart

20/6			
8 a.m.	...	...	99.4°
12 noon	...	...	99.2°
4 p.m.	...	...	101.2°
8 p.m.	...	...	100.2°
21/6			
8 a.m.	...	...	99°
11.30 a.m.	...	...	98.4°
4 p.m.	...	...	100°
8 p.m.	...	...	100°

At about 4 a.m.—heart pain, heavy perspiration, sinking feeling—temperature suddenly dropped. Temperature taken at

5.30 a.m.	...	...	97°
7 a.m.	...	...	180°
8 a.m.	...	...	98.2°

2

[Notes in Dr. Mookerjee's handwriting, in connection with his application before the Kashmir High Court]

1. See Sk. Abdullah's broadcast talk—where he refers to my arrest—and says I attempted to enter the state without a permit and courted arrest.
2. On 11th May J&K govt. passed an ordinance through the Sadar-i-Riyasat making it an offence for anyone to enter the state without a state permit. Please see this. My arrest was not under this ordinance.
3. There was no state law when I entered the state, requiring a permit. The G. of I. permit had apparently no legal validity—in any case the authorities in India did not arrest me for attempting to enter without their permit; rather, the D.C. of Gurudaspur received instructions to give me all facilities and not create any obstruction in case I decided to proceed to J&K without their permit.
4. J&K High Court has the jurisdiction to interfere. The law is special. It gives wide powers to the executive to arrest and detain a person for an unlimited period without giving him a charge-sheet and without having his case enquired into by any tribunal.
5. The words 'reasonably satisfied' give power to the court to intervene, if the circumstances of a case so warrant.

Compare the present Indian law. The Supreme Court has apparently no jurisdiction to go into the merits of a case of detention. But merely because the Act provides that grounds of detention are to be communicated to the internee to enable him to make representation, the Supreme Court has intervened and considered in many cases, whether the grounds are such as would give a fair opportunity to the accused to make his representation. It has proceeded on a liberal interpretation and has not refused to intervene merely because the Act gave powers to formulate its own grounds. Even if one ground is bad, the detention has been held illegal.

In this state this archaic, barbarous and lawless law still operates and the court, which cannot obviously go outside the four corners of the Act, can certainly step in, if it is satisfied on the facts of a particular case that there could possibly have been no application of 'reasonableness'.

"In any case, if in a case the surrounding circumstances show a malafide intention on the part of the executive, the court can certainly intervene. Malafide is suggested by the following:

1. My telegram to Abdullah and his reply—he did not then consider my visit to be so *dangerous* (it was *inopportune)* as to bring it within the scope of the P.S. Act.
2. Conspiracy between Government of India and J&K government—the circumstances under which my entry was facilitated by Indian officials.
3. Keeping both orders ready beforehand, specially the second order which, when signed, mentioned

certain alleged facts which could not possibly then be in existence.

4. The broadcast talk of Sk. Abdullah—declaring that my arrest was for entering the state without permit—which proves the reasons given in the orders served on me were unfounded.

Distinguish the court from the executive. The court should not stand on technicalities or narrow interpretation of law—but, as had been held in Supreme Court and other courts in all democratic countries—uphold personal liberty and not make it completely subservient to executive whims.

If reference is made to subsequent happenings in Jammu—leading to disturbances and arrest, you can say all this has been largely due to my arrest—if government had acted otherwise, the effect would have been different."

3

Petitions filed before the High Court of Kashmir with annexures (Order of Arrest & Detention)

IN THE HIGH COURT OF JAMMU & KASHMIR AT SRINAGAR

Criminal Miscellaneous Application

of......................2010

In the matter of Dr. Syama Prasad Mookerjee, a detenu

&

In the matter of Section 3(1) of the Public Security Act, 2003

&

In the matter of Section 491 of the Cr. Procedure Code
In the matter of Devki Prashad Nakhasi, petitioner
Versus ....1. Inspector-General of Police, Jammu & Kashmir Government
2. Superintendent, Central Jail, Srinagar

Respondents

The humble application of the petitioner above named respectfully showeth:—

1. That the detenu is a Member of the Parliament, an ex-Cabinet Minister of the Union Government and ex-Vice-Chancellor of the Calcutta University and is a citizen of India.
2. That the detenu was arrested by the police on 11.5.53 at Lakhanpur purporting to act under Section 3(1) of the Public Security Act 2003, under an order made by respondent No. 1.
3. That about 10 minutes before the said arrest, an order bearing No. 382-F/53 dated 10-5-1953 was served upon the detenu under Section 4(1) of Public Security Act, prohibiting him from entering, residing or remaining in any part of the state of Jammu & Kashmir on the allegation that the said detenu was about to act in a manner prejudicial to the public safety and peace in Jammu & Kashmir vide copy annexed marked 'A'.
4. That the said detenu has been kept in detention under the supervision of respondent No. 2, the Superintendent, Central Jail, Srinagar.

5. That the detenu has not been allowed to give full and free instructions to his advocate Shri U.M. Trivedi, barrister-at-law and hence further details of the nature of detention, conditions of detention, duration of detention and circumstances accompanying the detention could not be mentioned in this petition.
6. That Shri U.M. Trivedi did go to the place of detention on 12.6.53 at 5 p.m. but as he was told that the instructions could only be given in the hearing of the District Magistrate, Shri Trivedi refused to take such instructions and Dr. S.P. Mookerjee, the detenu refused to give such instructions.
7. That under the above circumstances, the application from the detenu himself was not possible and as the detenu has no relatives in Jammu & Kashmir state, the petitioner filed this application as his friend.
8. That the arrest of the said detenu and his detention is illegal and without any authority of law.
9. That no reasonable grounds existed or exist which can warrant the detention of the said detenu.
10. That the detenu never acted in any manner prejudicial to the peace or safety of the state.
11. That detention was malafide and preconceived as will be apparent from the order passed 10 minutes before the arrest of the detenu.
12. That the detenu is a citizen of India and his fundamental rights of freedom guaranteed by the Constitution of India under Article 19(d) has been so guaranteed to him as a citizen of India.

13. That the order served upon the said detenu before the arrest was also illegal and offended against the provisions of Article 19(e) of the Constitution.
14. That the respondent No. 1 had no grounds on which he could act much less had he any reasonable grounds for so acting and hence the order of arrest and detention passed by him is without proper authority and the continued detention without production before a magistrate is wholly unlawful.

Wherefore the petitioner prays that the respondents be ordered to produce the detenu before the Hon'ble Court and he be set at liberty thereafter.

AND SHALL EVER PRAY

Petitioner

Dated 15th June, 1953

IN THE HIGH COURT OF JAMMU & KASHMIR AT SRINAGAR

Criminal Miscellaneous application
of....................2010

In the matter of Dr. Syama Prasad Mookerjee, a detenu.
In the matter of Section 3(1) of the Public Security Act, 2003

&

In the matter of Section 491 of the Cr. Procedure Code

&

In the matter of Devki Prashad Nakhasi, petitioner.

Versus ....1. Inspector-General of Police, Jammu & Kashmir Government.

2. Superintendent, Central Jail, Srinagar.

Respondents

The application of the detenu above named respectfully showeth:

1. That he has read the application made by Shri Devki Prashad under Section 491 of the Criminal Procedure Code.
2. That before coming to Jammu & Kashmir, the detenu had intimated to Shri Sheikh Mohammad Abdullah by a telegram of his proposed visit and of the purpose of his visit, viz. to study the conditions himself and to explore the possibilities of creating conditions leading to peaceful settlement and to see if possible Hon'ble Shri Sheikh Mohammad Abdullah, and he had received a reply thereto which is annexed hereto and marked 'B'. The telegram which the said detenu sent from Amritsar was despatched on 8.5.53 and the aforesaid reply reached him at Phagwara on 9.5.53.
3. That he had entered the state with the full knowledge of the Indian authorities and in fact the Deputy Commissioner, Gurudaspur saw him at Pathankot on 11.5.53 and intimated to him that the authorities will not obstruct him and party from entering into Jammu & Kashmir although he and his party had no permits. The said Deputy Commissioner proceeded to the Madhopur check-post to see that his entry into the state without permit was facilitated.

4. That after he and his party had travelled by Jeep half way over Ravi, he was met by one Shri Capt. A. Azeez, S.P. of Kathua and served with an order prohibiting entry into the state, which has been marked 'A'. After apprising him of the circumstances leading to his entry into the state, he asked him to allow him to proceed to Jammu. Thereupon he immediately produced the order of arrest marked 'C' referred to previously and took him into custody. Both these orders, the said Capt. A. Azeez was carrying with him and the interval that lapsed between the communication of the first order and the second order was not more than a minute.

5. That simultaneously two of his companions Shri Guru Duttji and Shri Tek Chandji, who expressed their desire to accompany him were also later taken into custody but were served with no order on the spot but some order was read out to them at the Lakhanpur check-post where they had halted for an hour or so before his departure for Srinagar.

Wherefore the detenu prays that this may be read as part of the application and in addition thereto.

AND SHALL EVER PRAY,

Sd. Syama Prasad Mookerjee
Petitioner

Dated 18th June, 1953

In the High Court of Judicature Jammu & Kashmir, Srinagar.
Criminal Misc. No.. of 2010.

In the matter of Shri Devki Prashad ....Petitioner
Versus

1. Inspector-General of Police
2. Superintendent, Central Jail } Respondents

AFFIDAVIT

I, Syama Prasad Mookerjee, son of Sir Ashutosh Mookerjee, aged 52 years, now a detenu in a sub-jail at Srinagar, states on solemn affidavit as follows:

1. That the statements contained in paragraphs 1 to 5 in the accompanying application are true.
2. That I make this affidavit bonafide.

Sd. Syama Prasad Mookerjee,
Detenu

Solemnly affirmed before me at

Sd. G. Nabi
District Magistrate
18.6.53

(True copy)

'B'

Copy of a telegram dated 9th of May 1953 from Sheikh Mohammad Abdullah to Syama Prasad Mookerjee.

Thanks for your telegram—I am afraid your proposed visit to the state at the present juncture inopportune and will not serve any useful purpose.

Jammu & Kashmir Government

Order No. 382-F/53 of 1953 Dated 10-5-1953

To

Dr. Syama Prasad Mookerjee,
President, Bharatya Jan Sangh,
20 Tughlak Crescent,
New Delhi

Whereas the government are satisfied that there

are reasonable grounds for believing that you, Dr. Syama Prasad Mookerjee are about to act in a manner prejudicial to the public safety and peace of and in furtherance of the movement prejudicial to the public safety and peace in Jammu & Kashmir state;

And whereas it is necessary to prevent you from acting in the aforesaid manner,

Now, therefore, in exercise of the powers conferred by sub-section (1) of Section 4 of the Jammu & Kashmir Public Security Act, 2003, the government hereby directs that you Dr. Syama Prasad Mookerjee shall not enter, reside or remain in any part of the state of Jammu & Kashmir.

By order of the government,

Sd. Chief Secretary

ORDER

Whereas, I, Prithvinandan Singh, Inspector-General of Police, Jammu & Kashmir, am satisfied that there are reasonable grounds for believing that Dr. Syama Prasad Mookerjee, president, Bharatiya Jan Sangh, 30 Tughlak Crescent, New Delhi, has acted, is acting and is about to act in a manner prejudicial to public safety and peace, and whereas in order to prevent him from so acting in the aforesaid manner, it is necessary to make the following order:

Now, therefore, in exercise of the powers conferred on me by Section 3(1) of the Public Security Act, Act No. 15 of 2003 read with notification forming an annexure to Council Order No. 356-C of 1947, dated 20th May, 1947, I hereby order that the said Dr. Syama Prasad Mookerjee be arrested.

This is, therefore, to authorise and direct you, Captain A. Azeez, Superintendent of Police, Kathua, to arrest the said Dr. Syama Prasad Mookerjee and remove him under custody to Central Jail at Srinagar.

Herein fail not.

Given under my hand this 29th day of *Baisakh*, 2010, (11th of May 1953).

Sd. Inspector-General of Police
Jammu & Kashmir Government

Dated Lakhanpur
29.1.2010/11-5-1953

ORDER

Whereas, I, Prithvinandan Singh, Inspector-General of Police, Jammu & Kashmir, am satisfied that there are reasonable grounds for believing that Dr. Syama Prasad Mookerjee, president, Bharatiya Jan Sangh, 30 Tughlak Crescent, New Delhi, has acted, is acting and is about to act in a manner prejudicial to public safety and peace, and whereas in order to prevent him from so acting in the aforesaid manner, it is necessary to make the following order:

Now, therefore, in exercise of the powers conferred on me by Section 3(2) of the Public Security Act, Act No. 15 of 2003 read with notification forming an annexure to Council Order No. 356-C of 1947, dated 20th May, 1947, I hereby order that the said Dr. Syama Prasad Mookerjee be detained in custody at Central Jail, Srinagar for a period of two months.

This is, therefore, to authorise you, the Superintendent Central jail, Srinagar, to receive the said Dr. Syama Prasad Mookerjee and detain him in the Central Jail at Srinagar, Srinagr, for a period of two months.

Given under my hand this 29th day of *Baisakh*, 2010, (11th of May 1953).

Sd. Prithvinandan Singh,
Inspector-General of Police

Dated Lakhanpur
11.5.1953/29-1-2010

Appendix-III

Syama Prasad Mookerjee
1901-1953

1901 Born in Calcutta on July 6.

1921 Took B.A. degree with Honours in English from the Presidency College, Calcutta, standing 1st in Class I.

1922 Married to Sudha Devi on April 16.

1923 M.A. in Indian Vernacular, standing 1st in Class I.

1924 Stood 1st in Class I in B.L.; enrolled as an advocate of the Calcutta High Court. Elected Fellow of the Calcutta University. Appointed a member of the Syndicate to fill the vacancy caused by the death of Sir Asutosh in May.

1926 Left for England to study for the bar. Joined Lincoln's Inn. Represented Calcutta University at the Conference of Universities of the British Empire.

1927 Called to the English bar.

1929 Elected to the Bengal Legislative Council as a Congress candidate representing the Calcutta University.

1930 Resigned from the Council when the Congress decided to boycott the legislatures. Re-elected as an Independent candidate.

1933 Lost his wife.

1934 Vice-Chancellor, University of Calcutta, for two successive terms, 1934-38.
President, Post-Graduate Councils in Arts and Science for successive years.
Dean of the Faculty of Arts.
Member and then Chairman, Inter-University Board.

1935 Member of the Court and Council of the Indian Institute of Science, Bangalore.

1937 Elected to the Bengal Legislative Assembly under the reformed Constitution from the University constituency.

1938 D. Litt (honoris causa) conferred by the Calcutta University and L.L.D. (honoris causa) by the Benares Hindu University.
Nominated to the Committee of Intellectual Co-operation of the League of Nations as India's representative.

1939 Took a prominent part in the Calcutta session of the All-India Hindu Mahasabha.

1940 Working president of the All-India Hindu Mahasabha, 1940-44, also president of the Hindu Mahasabha, Bengal.

1941 Finance Minister, Bengal, from December 11, 1941 to November 20, 1942 in the second Fazlul Huq Progressive Coalition Ministry.
Bhagalpur session of the Mahasabha was banned by the government of Bihar. Dr. Mookerjee, as president, proceeded to Bhagalpur to defy the ban, was arrested and detained under the Defence of India rules and later released.
Took part in Cripps Mission deliberations.

1942 Resigned from the Ministry of Bengal as a protest

against the Governor's policy of repression in Midnapore and elsewhere in connection with August 1942 movement. Wrote to Lord Linlithgow, the then Viceroy, outlining tentative proposals for an Indo-British settlement and attempted to interview Mahatmaji in jail but was refused permission.

1943 Organised large-scale relief during the Bengal famine.

Presided over the Amritsar session of the All-India Hindu Mahasabha.

President of the Royal Asiatic Society of Bengal from 1943 to 1945.

1944 Founded an English daily, *Nationalist.*

Presided over the Bilaspur session of the All-India Hindu Mahasabha.

1945 Played an important part in guiding the students when they clashed with the authorities during the observance of the I.N.A. day in November. Taken seriously ill soon after.

1946 Elected to the Bengal Legislative Assembly from the University constituency.

The great Calcutta killing and widespread communal troubles. Stood firmly behind the people. Formed the Hindustan National Guard.

Cabinet Mission.

Elected a member of the Constituent Assembly from Bengal.

Dr. Mookerjee organised a movement which led to the retention of a portion of Bengal in the Indian Union.

1947 Government formed by Pandit Nehru on August 15. Dr. Mookerjee joined the Cabinet and took over the portfolio of Industries & Supplies.

Advised the Hindu Mahasabha Working Committee to give up politics after the attainment of Independence and turn to social and cultural activities.

President of the Mahabodhi Society.

1948 Mahatma Gandhi assassinated, January 30.

The suggestion to re-orientate its policy given several months ago was accepted by the Mahasabha on February 15, 1948.

1949 In January the relics of Sariputta and Moggalana, the disciples of Buddha, were handed over to him by Pandit Nehru on behalf of the Government of India.

In August, the Mahasabha rescinded its decision of February 15, 1948, and resolved to resume its political activities.

Dr. Mookerjee resigned from the Mahasabha Executive.

1950 Nehru-Liaquat Ali Pact.

On April 8, Dr. Mookerjee resigned from the Central Cabinet because of acute disagreement with the Prime Minister regarding the latter's policy of appeasement towards Pakistan. Devoted himself wholeheartedly to the cause of the refugees and made extensive tours for the relief and rehabilitation of the refugees.

1951 Organised a new political party called People's Party and charged the Government of India with appeasement of Pakistan. In October in Delhi, an all-India organisation called the Bharatiya Jana Sangh was formed under the presidentship of Dr. Mookerjee, which drew adherents from all parts of the country.

Vehemently opposed in Parliament, the passage of

the Indian Constitution Amending Bill restricting fundamental rights.

1952 Returned to Parliament in the General Election from South Calcutta constituency. Pressed hard and repeatedly in and outside the Parliament for a firm policy towards Pakistan.

Formed National Democratic Party as an Opposition Bloc in the Parliament.

In November joined the celebrations at Sanchi where the Buddhist relics were finally reposed. Visited Burma, Cambodia and other countries in Southeast Asia.

Presided over the Banga Sahitya Sammelan at Cuttack and Jan Sangh Conference at Kanpur.

1953 Frequent clashes with the government, and particularly with Mr. Nehru, for lending his support to the agitation on behalf of the Praja Parishad movement in Jammu for full integration of the state of Jammu & Kashmir with India. Protracted but infructuous correspondence with Messrs Nehru and Abdullah for mutual discussion and peaceful solution.

Arrested in Delhi in March for alleged violation of a ban on procession in Chandni Chowk and detained, but released by the orders of the Supreme Court on a habeas corpus petition.

Entered Kashmir on May 11 and was arrested and put under detention at Srinagar.

Died at Srinagar, while in detention; cremated in Calcutta on June 24.

□□□